Texas Fury

A TEXAS BADGE MYSTERY

Texas Fury

Dusty Richards
with Velda Brotherton

THORNDIKE PRESS
A part of Gale, a Cengage Company

GALE
A Cengage Company

GALE
A Cengage Company

Thorndike Press, a part of Gale, a Cengage Company.

Thorndike Press® Large Print Softcover Western.
The text of this Large Print edition is unabridged.
Other aspects of the book may vary from the original edition.
Set in 16 pt. Plantin.

LIBRARY OF CONGRESS CIP DATA ON FILE.
CATALOGUING IN PUBLICATION FOR THIS BOOK
IS AVAILABLE FROM THE LIBRARY OF CONGRESS.

ISBN-13: 978-1-4205-2706-3 (softcover alk. paper)

Published in 2025 by arrangement with Hat Creek, an imprint of Roan & Weatherford Publishing Associates, LLC.

To Dennis Doty, a good editor and
an even better friend.
Hope I done you proud with this one.

ACKNOWLEDGMENTS

To the whole gang at Oghma Communications and Roan & Weatherford Publishing Associates who never cease to amaze me with their talent, assistance, and joy of this business of creativity. Thanks to Casey Cowan, Dennis Doty, George Mitchell, Rachel Patterson, Laura Lauda, and my editors with this one, Bob Giel, Anthony Wood, and Amy Cowan. The list goes on. If you've been right there with me all the way, you know who you are. Love you all.

One

Rose should've known when she took the temporary job in Carlton that all would not go well. She wasn't cut out to be a sheriff. Too many rules. So, when the gunfire began before she even had a cup of coffee the first morning on the job, it really ruined a perfectly nice day. But, she should've known.

Colt in hand, she ran out the door, jumped off the boardwalk, and headed in the direction of all the hoopla. Down at the new mercantile that still smelled like fresh-cut lumber, a crowd gathered. Jeff Jefferson, owner and only employee, stood out front waving a shotgun.

"I been robbed. I been robbed." His shout carried far and wide.

"Put that thing away before you shoot someone." Running past him, she hollered again for him to put the shotgun down. Without slowing, she skidded around the corner through the livery barn and out the back door into the pasture where Cimarron grazed at the cost of two-bits a day, starting today. The bay looked up, saw her, and came running. He resented not being ridden and was more than ready to go.

"We have to hurry, boy." Without pausing, she turned and ran back to the livery, the big Andalusian right on her heels. Inside, she hefted the saddle across his back. He danced in anticipation. She settled him with soft words, cinched the belly latigo, and swung up. Dust from the hooves of the robbers' fleeing horses hung over the road headed out of town. On the way, one of the cowards shot out the windows of the Brand Iron Café.

Maize and Hector would be furious. They'd ordered that glass from Dallas and had it shipped down on the train. Then they hired Josiah to hand-paint the name of the café and *Come In and Set a Spell* across the top in red and blue. It sure was pretty. *Was,* is right. They'd be devastated.

She hoped no one was hit but left that for Doc Payne who hurried to attend a woman cut by flying glass. Rose had to catch up with these ruffians and make them pay for coming to her town and causing such a ruckus. She only had to tap Cimarron with her heels, and he stretched his long legs in pursuit. Soon the thieves were in sight. Two of them hunched forward riding madly, firing their guns into the air, and whipping their mounts one side then the other with their reins. Rode like blamed Indians, using only their legs to hang on. Cimarron gained on them till they were a ways out of town. They disappeared behind a stand of trees around the curve at Clear Creek. Riding flat-out, she rounded the corner, and next thing she knew, she was sitting in the dusty road, a rope around her middle with Cimarron standing nearby looking at her as if she ought to be ashamed she had let that happen.

"Okay mister, get up off the ground real slow like and give me your gun." One outlaw stood over her, from her perspective, looking ten feet tall. The other held their mounts.

Hair tucked beneath her Stetson, and wearing britches, she might look like a mister, but she resented it anyway.

"Sheriff Rose Parsons to *you,* boy." She staggered to her feet and dusted off the seat of her britches.

The outlaw laughed. "Why danged if she ain't a woman."

Before she could work her way loose, he

tied her wrists, the little snot nosed brat. He couldn't be old enough to vote.

"Why's a purty girl like you wear britches?" He grabbed her Stetson and put it on his head, dirty locks hanging out.

She'd hit him with a stick if she wasn't trussed up. Now she'd never be able to wear that hat again. Probably had lice, dirty as he was.

A younger version of his dirty self jumped up and down, sending his horse dancing. "You roped her, by gum! You roped her! Boy howdy! Never saw that before."

The oldest one took over. "Chip, stop fooling around. Take off her boots and drag her over there against that rock before you bind her ankles. Then she can't hop away. And take the lasso off her. I gotta go to the woods." He looked around. "Reckon where Rick and Junior got to. They should already be here."

"Don't know. What'cha gonna do in the woods, Pete?"

"Ain't none of your business, kid. Just do what I told you, and I'll be right back."

"Why in thunder we stopping here? We ain't far enough from town yet."

The older one hit him with Rose's hat. Her good Stetson. "Shut up. If anyone was gonna follow us, they'd done been here. Jest a bunch of idjits. Who'd hire a woman sheriff anyway?"

Why didn't they shut up? At the moment, Rose wasn't feeling too kindly. "Don't you know it's against the law to hogtie a member of law enforcement? Get the rope off me before I enforce that law and drag you all off to jail."

Interrupting the muffled laughter at her words, two men who must be Rick and Junior rode out of the trees and joined in the merriment. They were all young. The one they called Chip looked to be just a kid, too young to shave. Acted like this was a game. Were they just starting their outlaw career? Well, she was about to put an end to it.

"What next, Rick?" The young one fairly danced with excitement, his eyes flashing while he looked all around. "Can we turn her loose and rope her again?"

"Don't be stupid. Let's get out of here before they send a posse after her."

The bigger one of the crew named Pete snatched Rose, threw her over Cimarron's saddle on her stomach. The pain sent a noisy grunt out that made them laugh. Pete returned buttoning his fly. They all mounted up and rode off, Pete leading her horse. After a while, the bouncing hurt Rose like the very devil. If she ever got her hands on these little thieves, she'd figure out all the punishments she could lay on them. They were only kids, and she would like to give them all a sound whipping. If they already had a bounty on their heads, then she could throw them in jail. Soon as she got loose.

That night, the gang finally stopped riding and set up camp along the banks of the river under some trees. Chip was put in charge of her, and he slid her off the saddle, staggered backward, and they both went on the ground, her lying on her back on top of him. It must've hurt him worse than her. Rick and Pete laughed so hard they couldn't finish building a fire and starting supper for some time.

Pete handed his horse's reins to Junior. "Put up a line and take care of our mounts. I don't want to wake up on foot."

Junior spared him a frown, but he did what he was told, except Cimarron didn't. He reared over the slight young man, hooves coming down close enough to topple his hat off. The huge Andalusian then ran off a ways, and every time the kid tried to get near, he darted off. The boy cursed.

"Leave him be," Pete and Rick both hollered.

After he took care of the horses, Junior

spent his time leaning against a tree paring his nails with a knife and giving her an ornery stare. He might've been the oldest of the four, but they were all under twenty if she had to guess. He was by far the meanest, with a vicious glint in his eye that gave him a devilish look. She wouldn't want to tangle with him.

The meal consisted of a couple cans of beans and two of peaches they bragged about stealing from the mercantile and some cornbread they praised someone named Mama for baking. They didn't give Rose anything.

"That's okay, dumb bunnies. I don't want food that's been stolen." She closed her eyes and leaned on the tree.

"Hey, all we stole was the beans and peaches. Mama sent the cornbread with us when we left home this morning."

"Mama? What would your ma think of you stealing . . . wait, you took a chance of getting shot for two cans of beans and peaches? Maybe you ought to rethink your career choice."

"Will you two shut up? I can't even think." Junior shook his head and crammed a spoonful of beans in his mouth. "And she's our gramma, not our ma, who died on us, which Mama said was big of her."

Later, Pete offered her the blanket off his horse to lie on when they bedded down for the night. When their snoring filled the night, she wiggled around till she could get a hand in the back pocket of her britches. Then she fingered out her pocketknife, worked it open and sawed her way out of her predicament. It never occurred to them to search her. Must not have believed a woman might carry a knife.

There was no moon, and the night was so black she couldn't see much of anything. Kept running into bushes and trees, so she finally hid out under an overhang in a wash until the sky lit enough she could make out shadows. Then she took out for Carlton. She hated leaving her horse on his own, tied like he was with the other four, but he'd go home first chance he had. Junior slept right near them, and she'd sure wake him up if she tried to get the bay.

The sun climbed in the cloudless sky, and by the time it was overhead, she was well away and sweating. Cuts in her bare feet were bleeding, and she wished mightily for Cimarron. Another couple hours and she could no longer bear walking on the searing hot sand. Clumps of grass offered some relief, and she hopped on an occasional rock which was nearly as hot as the sand.

A lizard wiggled from under a sandstone, tilted its head to study her closely, lids opening and closing over red-slit eyes.

Probably wanted to know where her boots were. *Well, Mr. Nosy, they're back yonder in that camp where those men with guns in their hands are tramping all around kicking the coffee pot and throwing all my stuff from the saddlebag. Do they honestly think I could hide anything of value there? I don't even own anything of value except Cimarron, and by now he'd gone home.*

And here she was talking to a lizard who had already lost interest and slithered under a king-sized boulder where she took refuge in its shadow. Cooling her feet in the patch of shade cast across the gritty sand, she peered in the direction of the four ruffians and hoped she could stay ahead of them. No doubt they wouldn't come after her and risk meeting up with a posse out of Carlton. No sense them risking jail for a few cans of beans and peaches. Chasing outlaws for the theft of some cans of food no longer made much sense either. If it got out, she'd never live it down.

At least she was loose and fleeing for her life from men not worth the bullets it'd take to blow them to Hell. Bullets she didn't have at the moment 'cause her revolver was down there in the hands of someone called Pete. Ah, well, she'd been wanting one of those Army Colt .44s. Now she had an excuse to get herself one. Do her no good at the moment. Dream on, though.

Shaking some sense back into her head, she imagined what they were doing by now. They knew she was gone, and Junior was cussing up a storm, the rest of them talking about whether to try to find her and kill her or to just ride on.

How in thunder had she got in this predicament?

Well, first thing, two weeks ago she'd delivered train robber Green Land to U.S. Deputy Marshal Joseph Banks in Amarillo, collected the bounty, and headed toward her new home in Carlton where she'd bought a small cabin on the riverbank. At the moment, Carlton was without a sheriff or town marshal, and Sheriff Dell Hoffman from over in Thomas City had talked her into hanging around to sort of protect the place till they could get someone willing to serve.

"There's just too many outlaws like to gather when a town is unprotected. Think they can run the place and get rich from the earnings," he told her.

So, she settled there. It surely wouldn't be

more than a few weeks before someone would come along wanting the job. That's how she came to be out here on her first day as sheriff, barefoot and hiding from four smart-ass baby outlaws who'd robbed the mercantile of two cans of beans and two more of peaches. Her, a bounty hunter who should have all four of them tied up and on the way to the nearest marshal's office for her money. They probably weren't even on the wanted list yet.

Sometimes things just didn't work out.

Dell Hoffman, sheriff of Saddler County, relaxed on the bench outside his office in Thomas City. An overhang sheltered him from the hot Texas sun. It felt danged good not to be out chasing some fool who couldn't obey simple laws. Instead, he watched Miss Lula Mae Hodges, the new schoolteacher, prance across the street, the tail of her dress swishing up dust in her wake. Made him feel good to watch folks going about their business. Safe. Behaving.

Just as he got danged sure of himself, folks began to scatter one way and another down the street. Some lady hollered to look out and from the melee ran that big Andalusian of Rose Parsons.

"What in the world?" No one on him

when he slowed and trotted right up to where Dell sat.

He stretched to his feet. The horse wasn't saddled but had a bit in its mouth and reins tied over his neck. Dell clicked his tongue and approached him slowly. He appeared spooked about something. He ran his hand down each leg, examined the hoof, moved all around talking softly.

Looping the reins back over his neck he led him down the street to the livery. Maybe Rose was in town and somehow Cimarron had decided to take a little walk. Both ought to be down in Carlton taking care of business. The livery stables and pasture were the very last business in town right across from the smithy, so he passed plenty of curious people who wanted to know what was wrong. It took a while to reach the wide open door where Joe Maples was seeing to a wagon.

Without glancing up from his work he greeted Dell. "Howdy, Sheriff. Sure is a hot one today, ain't it? Come on in out of the sun. Reckon what that bay of Rose's is doing in town?" He laid down his tools and stood on long thin legs that resembled sticks.

"Hoping you'd know something, Joe. He come through town like his tail was on fire.

She's supposed to be in Carlton. She didn't bring him in?"

Joe spit a stream of tobacco juice against the wagon wheel. "Nope, ain't seen her since last Sunday. Didn't she take the sheriff's job down there? Don't reckon she's already in trouble. I've said many a time no woman ought to be a bounty hunter and sure as shootin' needn't try sheriffing. Now here she's gone and doin' both." He shook his head.

"Well, I expect I ought to have Curly carry me on down to Carlton. See what's up. She's a tough little gal, but she could need some help. Surely that bay of hers ain't smart enough to come to fetch help?" Joe's attitude about Rose being sheriff irritated Dell, but he left it at that.

Rose had pitched right in the previous year when they were hunting that arsonist.

Joe dropped the tack on a bench and fetched Curly, the strong gelding sorrel the town had gifted Dell with after his own beloved horse was killed during a gunfight. The horse had a flaxen curly mane, thus the name.

While Joe muttered on about his favorite gripes, Dell saddled Curly and, leading Cimarron, headed for the house to tell Guinn where he was going. Even before he reined up at the front porch, he smelled bread baking. She was the best cook in the county and especially excelled in bread. Maybe there'd be a loaf ready and he could make a quick sandwich before he took off. Dinner time would be past when he got down there, took care of business, and rode home.

Guinn put together his requested sandwich. "I sure hope nothing has happened to Rose. I worry about her being sheriff in Legend County. There's some wild goin's on down there."

"Ah, Rose is a strong gal. She'll be okay. That horse of hers sometimes has a mind of his own, and he's been up here a lot. Probably just taking a walk."

She handed him the sandwich wrapped in butcher's paper, stood on her tiptoes, and kissed him on the cheek. He hugged her with one arm and returned the kiss to the top of her head.

"You be careful yourself. I'll keep supper warm for you."

He nodded. "I'll be back quick as I can."

Out on the trail, the sun climbed to noon time. Dust devils kicked up, and the hot Texas wind kept blowing. His sweat-soaked shirt clung to his back, but Dell was used to the heat in the panhandle of Texas. He wouldn't live anywhere else. Relaxing on the easy riding Curly, he unwrapped his sandwich and ate it while they plodded along. Damn, it was good. His favorite. Ham and Guinn's homemade cheese with mustard between slices of homemade bread warm from the oven. When he finished, he opened the canteen and washed it down with well water still cold from the bucket.

He rode up to the sheriff's office in Carlton hoping to see Rose out and about. Dismounting, he tied the horses to the hitch rail, took the steps to the boardwalk, and went inside. The place was empty. No one in the cells either. Back outside, with a sense of dread, he hailed a fellow riding down the street.

"You seen Rose today?"

"Not today. Yesterday evening she rode out of here after a couple of boys who robbed the mercantile and busted out the glass of the Brand Iron. Come to think of it, they was headed your way. Haven't seen her today, but surely she got that settled. They didn't look much out of short pants, so she could've sent them home with their britches tanned." He chuckled. "Heard all they took was some canned stuff, but they did bust that window glass down at the cafe. I'd say she's run into something else. Isn't that her horse you've got there? I sure do hope nothin's happened."

"Me, too. Yep, this is Cimarron. When was this? Early?"

"Coming on dinner time."

"Thanks." Well, damn and blast. Had she gone and gotten into trouble she couldn't get out of already? In her first week as temporary sheriff? If her quarry didn't reach Thomas City, they probably took the cut off to Hawkins Post, a fair piece. Julio Jenkins, his Apache friend, served as town marshal over there. Julio and his cousin, Angelo, both Apache blood, were the only lawmen in the small town near the Territorial border. Dang it was hot out and only got hotter in that direction. Since the railroad passed through all these towns, there was a telegraph here in Carlton as well as Hawkins Post, so, rather than ride out, he'd send a wire first.

Tabor Jones looked up from under the brim of his head guard. "Help ye?"

"I need to send a wire to Julio over in Cactus Junction."

Tabor pushed a tablet over to him. "Write, can ye?"

Dell grinned, wondered what a telegraph written by this man would read like. "Yes sir, I can." He took up the fat pencil and adjusted the paper to write his message. Licking the tip, he set it on the paper just as the fellow he'd met earlier came running from the livery, sweat pouring over his face.

"Sheriff, glad I caught you." He panted a few breaths. "Doc Payne, he found Rose." More panting and wiping of his face with his bandana.

Dell wanted to shake it out of him, this important news about Rose. "Well, go on. Is she hurt? Where is she? Spit it out."

The fellow pointed up the street toward the edge of town.

Dell didn't wait for more words. He just took off, leaving Curly and Cimarron standing there. In front of the Brand Iron Café, a huddle of people milled about. He couldn't make out what they were looking at. What if it were Rose, laying there dead? And him to blame for putting her on the job.

He shoved his way through the women in their fat skirts and men stretching to see past those in front of them.

"Out of the way, get out of my way. Sheriff here. Move it."

Finally, he made it past everyone to where Doc knelt over a figure in britches and bright blue shirt lying on her belly in the dirt, a fan of sweat soaked golden hair spread about her head.

He dropped to his knees. "Good Lord, Doc. Is she dead?"

"No, I'm not dead, you old fool." Rose's voice muttered so he could barely hear it over the loud conversations going on in the crowd.

"Someone done shot our sheriff." A coarse male voice declared.

"Is she dead?" A trembling woman's voice asked.

"For goodness sake, move these people back and give her some air." Doc turned to Dell. "Take charge of these folks so I can tend to her, would you, Sheriff?"

Wishing he could touch her to see if she were indeed alive, Dell came out of his distraction and rose to his feet with a mighty surge. Pulling his six-shooter, he aimed it high and pulled the trigger.

The crowd stirred, moved a bit, then turned and took off when he waved the thing around and hollered. "Go on, git about your business so Doc can assess this woman."

People fled in every direction, declaring their feelings in no uncertain terms. Good thing he wasn't running for sheriff in this town, or they'd not vote for him. Just the same, Dell was glad he'd taken charge, even if he did scare some of the women till they turned white and shook their heads in anger.

Doc grumbled. "That's better. Now let's see to this little gal."

Two

Rose found herself lying face down in the street, dirt sticking to her sweat-soaked clothes and not sure how she got there. Her feet ached, her skin burned, and she was worn out till she could hardly move. Dell and Doc both talked to her, but she could hardly respond. Though mightily ashamed, she tried to tell them about that gang of kids who'd kept her prisoner into the night. Even though she finally broke loose and ran, she could barely speak between deep breaths. Every inch of her body hurt. And no wonder, after getting walloped on she had spent the night running and laying on the ground for over twenty miles, and she hated to run anyway.

"Be easy, girl. I'm going to turn you over." Doc moved her gently and brushed long strands of hair from her face.

She opened her eyes and struggled to sit up, tried to say something — *anything* — to explain why she lay in the street exhausted.

But nothing would come.

"Just a minute there, girl, till we see just where you're hurt. Are you shot anywhere?"

"No, no." Two words. Well, she was doing better. She shifted her gaze to a blurry Dell. "Hello, Sheriff. Water?"

He jumped as if startled. "Water. Of course I'll get you some, Doc?"

Doc pointed at the café. "In there, son. They have water."

"Oh, sure. Be right back. Don't let her get up yet."

"I'm the doctor, go get the water. Come on, Rose. Nothing seems broken. Let's see if you can sit." He put an arm around her shoulder and lifted easy like. "Anything hurt?"

She rubbed her arms. "Only my dignity. I just need to get out of this dirt and maybe lay down somewhere clean."

Dell returned with a glass of water, and she drank it in huge gulps, handed it back. "More please."

"Not yet, girl. Let's get you put inside. Then you can have more water. You don't want to founder."

"Doc, people don't founder. Only animals do that." She was getting herself back from wherever one went when in the shape she'd been in. It was a weird feeling, like all sense had fled from her body then dropped her in an unfamiliar place where she could no longer make sense of anything.

With Dell on one side and Doc on the other, they took her in the café where Hector and Maizie insisted she go in the back room where they had a cot and lie down for a while. Rose was glad to do that. "But bring me some more water, if you would."

Maizie laughed. "I'll also bring you a wash pan and help you can clean up a bit. Looks like you've had quite an adventure. You'll have to tell us about it."

Knowing it would be all over town by supper time, Rose prepared to tell her sorry tale. She could always add a few exciting details. Maybe make herself look brave.

She remained with Maizie a while after Doc and Dell left, and Hector returned to serving customers.

"You know, Doc, this makes the second time Carlton has had a problem with children acting up. We need to get this problem taken care of in a hurry."

Doc agreed with Dell. "From what Rose said, they are too young to be out doing whatever they please. It's like a game to them, and they need to understand someone will get hurt even worse."

"I'm not sheriff of this county, but I'm going to go round them up. Maybe we can find somewhere for them to live and work and act responsible." He went back and told Rose what he intended to do. "I hope you can identify these little buggers if I bring them in."

"Oh, I can, but I'm not up to helping you catch them yet."

Dell stared at her. "Well, girl, I'm glad you're being sensible about this. It's the first time I've known you to back off from anything. Those boys must've put the fear of God in you."

She shrugged and looked away, not willing to say more. Hard to admit kids had got the better of her. Scared her, in fact. "I'll stay here and let you handle it, but be careful, they just look innocent."

"Not that I'm afraid of them or anything," she told Maizie after Dell left. "I just think, though I hate to say it, taking care of this is not a woman's job but a man's. Mostly 'cause those boys won't listen to words from a female. They need a good walloping. And I sure couldn't take a gun to them. They're just kids but awful mean ones."

She spent the remainder of that day in the sheriff's office taking care of paperwork. There was a lot to do since Sheriff Gus

Talken had been gunned down. The lone deputy had resigned, and his papers had to be filed, and the town marshal was out of the county on business. Her own papers had not been filled out, and she'd been putting that off because she'd hoped someone would come along to take the job. It was time she got on the trail again, where grown men who broke the law could be pursued and shot if they didn't surrender.

Leafing through all the wanted posters to find so many outlaws riding free convinced her of that, but she couldn't go back on her promise to carry out the duties as Carlton's sheriff for now. Perhaps there'd be some in the posters that she as the local sheriff could pursue. Of course, she'd sworn to guard and protect the people of Saddle County, so that came first. Maybe she could find someone who would qualify for her attention.

A couple of those shown on posters appeared to do just that. One outlaw, along with an unknown helper, had escaped the local jail almost a year earlier. The two of them had been engaged in stealing cattle from ranchers in the county. Just a few here, and a few there, until they had a nice-sized herd, then driving them down to a port city where they were shipped out of the country.

The notes Talken had made included his

opinion that these two yahoos thought if they kept each robbery to four or five head, the rancher wouldn't miss them for a while, and no one would be looking for cattle thieves. Someone had given a description of one of the men who had been overheard talking about their feat in the Mule Shoe Saloon here in town. But other than that, no one seemed to know anything about the cattle thefts.

She studied the crude drawings of the outlaws' features for a long time because one vaguely resembled Wade Guthrie, who had charmed her and became one of the wanted outlaws she didn't take in. At the time, his bounty was only two hundred dollars. A paltry sum compared to being in his arms briefly. The amount on the poster for this man was a thousand dollars. If this truly was his description and he'd been stealing cattle, then his charms weren't worth that.

At the moment, the only problem was, as sheriff, she couldn't collect the bounty. The more she studied the poster, the more convinced she was it was truly Wade. The description of his helper was so vague as to be useless, but he was worth another five hundred. He must not be as active in the enterprise. She folded the wanted poster and locked it in a drawer of the desk. Maybe tomorrow or the next day she could find a candidate for sheriff and then could pursue Wade Guthrie and earn that thousand dollars. She sure hated to think of him locked away though. But as sheriff, it would take months to earn that much.

By evening, with the exception of sore feet, she felt better. She limped around the entire town, checking each business to see the doors were locked and nothing looked out of place. By dark everything looked good. The three saloons were open and doing big business, but nothing was out of hand. Ever since that arsonist had burned the mercantile last year, everyone in town had learned how important it was to pitch in and help each other, so it was pretty peaceful. That was one of the reasons she'd agreed to hold down this temporary appointment. No reason to get impatient, this was only her third day on the job.

Yeah, sure, and the first two were spent tied up by four boys playing dangerous games. And thinking of that, where was Dell? He should've been back hours ago with those kids in tow. Would she have to go out and rescue him? On the way to the Mule Shoe, she spotted one of the men she'd seen with her cousin, Jake, at Palo Duro Canyon last year. He was with an older man she didn't know. When they went inside the saloon, she followed.

Time for her to indulge in one glass of beer and relax a bit. The town appeared tied down good. She nodded at Jeff Jefferson and saw Hector who sat with the sign painter, Josiah. Doc Payne was having what looked like whisky at a table by himself. Bart Black and Tabor Jones were sitting in on a poker game in the back corner. Obviously this was one of the more popular saloons in town. She'd heard that an entirely different group hung out at the new place on the edge of town where cowboys, out of work and cowboys with work, mingled. Lightning Strike was what they'd named it, but that was a mite dumb, like daring such a thing to happen there.

Looking around, it was obvious that if she wanted to find someone to take over being sheriff, she was in the wrong place. The new one attracting out of work cowboys. That was where she ought to be.

Before she could leave, Doc spotted her. "Come on over here and join me, young lady. Let me make sure you survived your ordeal okay."

She smiled and went to sit with him. He needed to know she was all right. The bartender eyed her, and she ordered a beer.

Doc peered at her in the gloom of the room, lit by lamps hung around on the walls. "You look pretty good. How do you feel?"

"Humiliated. Ridiculous, incompetent. Let's see, my feet hurt, but I feel fine otherwise."

Doc smiled and took a sip of his whisky. The bartender brought her beer and sat it down. "Had yourself quite a day or two, huh, Sheriff? Don't reckon if we had a man in office that would've happened. No offense intended."

"None taken. All the same, that's bullshit. Four against one in any situation is tough to beat." She grinned at him as if they were discussing the weather. "Maybe you'd like to quit your job and run for sheriff? Then you could show me how to handle four rough armed kids. Only a suggestion."

He nodded. "Yes, ma'am. Anything else?"

"No thanks."

"I guess you told him." Doc tilted his glass and finished the drink. Rising, he touched her hand. "Take care a day or two. Something like that can cause more problems than you expect."

She nodded, finished off her beer, and stood. "I'll walk with you a spell, if you don't mind."

He tipped his head forward as if in a bow. "Don't mind at all."

Doc lived over the drug store behind his office and exam rooms. He left her at the stairs alongside the building. A dark alley ran on to the back. When the two of them stopped to say goodnight, a man stepped out.

"Doctor Payne. Are you . . . ?" He slumped over the stair railing. "I'm afraid I've been shot." The words came out between gasps.

"Get his arm, Rose." Doc grabbed the other. "Let's get him upstairs before he passes out."

Her hands around his arm slipped in something warm and sticky. "He's bleeding over here."

"How much? Pulsing or oozing?"

"I can't really tell in the dark."

"Put a finger on it."

She did, thinking that sounded strange. "Oh, Doc, I can feel it coming out. Pulsing, like you said."

"Come on then, let's get him up." He had gone several steps while telling her to check the bleeding, and they managed to get the good-sized man through the door and onto the exam table before he collapsed.

With her assistance, Doc cleaned the

wound and bound it tightly to stop the bleeding. "Bullet went clean through. He should be all right if it doesn't get infected. Do you recognize him?"

She studied the whiskered face in light from the lamp. "Nope. Just another out of work cowboy. Probably indulging in a gunfight down in Cactus Junction. From what I've seen, there lots of men like him end up hanging around there."

"Yeah, it's too bad so many men around here are out of work. With cattle prices so low, ranchers just can't pay a big crew, and they're getting by with fewer men."

"Is that why? I never pay attention to things like that."

Doc felt the man's forehead with the back of his hand. "A little warm, I'll keep an eye on him overnight."

She nodded. "I'm thinking of going up to Lightning Strike and poking around for someone who might take the sheriffing job so I can get on the road again."

"Getting bored, are you?" He grinned. "Ever think of settling down, getting married, and having a houseful of kids?"

"Lord no, I'd go out of my mind staying in one house more than a week or two. As for kids, I'd be the worst momma in the world." She glanced at the sleeping man.

"Not bad looking like some who come through."

"You be careful at that place."

"Doc, I'm safer there than I was with those four young yahoos. I know what to do to defend myself with grown men."

He whispered a laugh. "I reckon you do, girl. Well, I'll wait up for those who tangle with you."

"Funny, Doc. You're plumb funny."

Bad as he hated it, Dell Hoffman had to do something he hadn't resorted to in ages. He got in a fistfight with two of the boys. It didn't last long. He knocked the oldest one on his butt with one roundhouse blow, turned and threw the other to the ground knocking the wind out of him. Standing over the two of them, he remained silent for a minute while they recovered enough to listen.

"Now, let's talk. You two brothers?"

They nodded.

"Where's the other two?"

The one with the bloody nose pointed behind them. "And if they'd been here, you'd been sorry, 'cause you'd a been on the ground."

"Where you boys come from?"

"Here and there. Mostly Texas, though."

This, from the smaller one.

"A big state. *Where,* I asked? You'd be smart to answer my questions in a mannerly way before I turn you over my lap and whip your butts."

"Oh, yeah? We ain't babies. You cain't whup us."

"Well, so far you haven't done so well. What's your name, boy?"

The kid glared at him. "You wait till Pete and Junior get here. They'll show you how the cow ate the cabbage."

Dell dug in his saddlebag, took out slips of rope, and tied their wrists out in front of them so they could ride sitting rather than being thrown over their saddles. The small one kicked and screamed to no avail, but the older one glared daggers at him and said nothing. Murder in his eyes. Easy to see why Rose had a problem handling these boys. Where had the other two gotten to? For that matter, where were their horses? They must have them, but Rose didn't say.

"Boy, where's your horses?" He shook the older of the two.

"Guess you'd like to know, you old buzzard."

"Hush that mouth of yours. Guess you're gonna *walk* back to Carlton. You can run alongside my fine Curly here. Does that suit you?"

He took his rope off his saddle, looped it through those on their wrists and climbed in the saddle. "Let's go, Curly."

The sorrel loped off, the two boys running and yelling, kicking up dust and pebbles. After a while, when they'd had enough, he halted Curly. The boys hunched over, breathing heavily. "We getting anywhere with this yet, or should I tell old Curly here to flat out gallop?"

They looked at each other, sweat pouring through the dust coating their face. "You about ready to act human?" He didn't want to run them till they were sick, but they were sure stubborn.

The young one broke then, covered his face with bent elbow and began to cry. Dell almost felt sorry for him. No telling how they'd been brought up, but somewhere, sometime, they had to be taught to get along in this world, or someone would gun them down before they really had a life.

Dell dismounted and took the boys by the arms and walked them into the shade under a lone tree alongside the trail. "Let's sit here a while and see if we can't figure this out. You want to keep running beside my horse, or you want to ride yours? Up to you."

The young one hiccoughed and looked at his older brother. "We'll ride for now, but when Pete and Junior get to you —"

Dell cuffed him across the arm. Hit him hard enough to get his full attention. "I'll do the same to them only worse. How old you boys? If you're over fourteen, you'll go to jail. You assaulted a sheriff. Who taught you to be so downright stupid?"

"Mister! Hey, mister! Git away from my brothers, right now."

A bullet cut the dust near Dell. He jumped aside. He'd been a fool, not paying attention to his surroundings. The little bastard had sneaked up on him, and he was lucky to be alive. He got his bearings and glared toward the sound of the voice. Two boys, one ever bit as big as him but without a shadow of whiskers, stood a few feet away, holding a rifle still pointed in Dell's direction.

"You'd best put that rifle down, boy, 'fore someone gets hurts."

"It's bound to be you, 'less you untie my brothers and let 'em come over here to me."

Caught in a blamed impossible situation, Dell untied the boys. "You two remember what I said. It's gonna be a hard road for you if you keep going in this direction."

The one with the rifle hollered at him,

"Hey, you old son of a bitch. Stop talking that rot to my brothers and let 'em come to me. I'll leave you then and not kill you this time."

Dell shoved the two boys away, then turned to stare down the other two. "You ever kill anyone?"

"Not yet, but I'm fixin to kill *you* if you don't shut your mouth."

"I pray you never are foolish enough to do so. It'll haunt you the rest of your life."

The boy spit in the dirt and grabbed the bigger of his two brothers, began to shake him. Curse him. Bare his teeth at him. Then he kicked him in the seat of his pants.

"Go on back there and get our horses, you useless ass."

Dell shook his head in dismay. One day he might be the one to have to shoot one of these boys when he'd have no other choice. He'd met grown men easier to reason with than these kids.

The boy then turned back to Dell, who stood near Curly. He held out a dirty hand. "Give me those reins."

"What?"

"I want that purty horse. Give me the reins."

This was where he'd draw the line. "You'll have to take him."

"Maybe I'll shoot you and take him."

Dell gritted his teeth. He couldn't let that happen. This kid had no idea what it would do to him to shoot someone, especially if he died. So, he turned sideways, held out the reins, and, when the boy started forward, he drew his gun, and his first shot cut the dirt between the boy's feet. Another did the same with the brother who stood closest. The boys both danced and yelped.

"Before you point that rifle at me, I want you to think about something. Think how fast my finger will pull this trigger again, and I always hit what I aim at." Dear God, how could he even consider shooting a young man such as one of these? Yet he saw no way out of it if the boy didn't put down the rifle and walk off. He was willing to let him do that.

The boy took a step sideways as if he were going to run, which Dell would have allowed at this point, rather than shooting him. But he didn't run. Instead he brought up the rifle and aimed it at Dell.

Both shots sounded so close together, Dell wasn't sure he had fired until the boy went down. Looked like he just melted into his old, ragged high-top shoes and lay still as death.

Dell let out a breath and stared through

tear dimmed eyes at the distant horizon, unable to look at the kid lying in the dirt.

Three

On his knees in the dirt, Dell held the boy, his own tears staining the ragged old shirt the kid wore. "Lord Jesus, why? *Why?*"

He'd not had time to aim when the kid turned on him. Just faced the bore of that rifle and knew without a doubt the boy was about to kill him. He'd hoped he could stop him. There was no time for anything but to fire at him and hope to God he only winged him.

He laid his hand flat over the bloody chest. But he'd killed him, just like that. In the snap of his fingers, in the bat of his eyes, he'd killed a child.

An image of his child, dying in Guinn's arms and him unable to do anything but hold the two of them, hit him like a brutal wind. His stomach roiled, his heart banged, his head throbbed, and the tears wouldn't stop. He'd warned the kid what it would be like to kill someone. And this was it. Damn how he hated this. Beyond words.

The younger of the brothers lay in the dust behind Dell crying. The other two held each other and promised all sorts of things would happen to Dell.

After a long time, he moved the boy to the grass under the shade tree, untied the two, and, ignoring the other one shouting vengeance at the top of his lungs, mounted up. "You three go or stay or whatever. I'm going to notify the first lawman I see about this." He swung a limp arm in the direction of the dead boy. "I'm sorry about your brother, I truly am. Never draw down on an armed man."

Neither of the three uttered a word when he rode away. He was almost out of sight when one yelled, "We'll get you for this, puke face. You'll see."

He rode into Hawkins Post before he found a lawman. Julio Jenkins sat on the porch alongside his cousin, Angelo. Weary and saddened by circumstances, he only lifted a hand when they called out to him. Tying Curly at the hitching post, he scuffed up the steps and stood before them, head hanging for a silent moment, before he said anything.

"I've killed me a child. Yonder." He pointed up the trail. Covering his eyes with a spread hand, he wept.

Julio patted him on the back then took him inside. Angelo followed, asked how far without any other words. Dell shook his head. "No more'n a few miles this side of Carlton."

"Angelo, stay here with him." He gestured, took his cousin aside. "Do not let him out of your sight till I get back."

"Is he arrested?"

Julio studied the boards between his feet. Nodded. "He has to stay till we get the body and a report is made. Otherwise he will be hunted down. Do what you have to."

Dell shuffled into the office, stepped into the only cell, and closed the door before slumping onto the bunk. There he held his face in both hands to quiet the sobs that erupted from his very heart and soul.

Julio cleared his throat. "Dell, I'm not locking you up for this. I just need you here until I return."

Dell nodded, tried to speak, couldn't, just nodded again, waved a hand to send him on his way. Long after Julio left, he remained in that very spot, thinking about vengeance and killing and the human kind. Finally, weary to the very bones, he swiveled to lie down on the hard bunk and close his eyes. But he couldn't sleep for the demons that darted through his mind.

It was almost dark when Julio returned. He stomped dust off his boots, then came in the office. Angelo spoke in his singing cadence. "He has not moved, but I do not believe he sleeps."

Alerted by the conversation, Dell took a deep breath to ready himself for whatever was to come. It couldn't be worse than what had already happened.

But it was.

"I found the spot. There's blood on the ground, but there is no body. Nor is there anyone there to tell us what happened. We must go by the marks, and they only show turmoil, struggle, and blood. We cannot know someone died there. What do you want us to do? I can file a report on the incident."

The incident, said so coldly, tore at him. Somehow he'd known in his heart that the boys would carry their brother away, that they would want to avenge his death rather than letting the law take care of it. The law would have called it self-defense. This he knew. But those boys would never settle for that. And he wondered if he ever would. No matter how he went over and over what happened, he could not see a different way, yet he had killed a child, and he could never forgive himself.

"I think I'd like to file the report. There are no witnesses save the other three brothers, and they won't come forward." He spread his hands, studied the fingers one by one. Shook his head fiercely.

"If you need anything, let us know. Do we have wanteds on these boys?" The big Apache pulled out his desk drawer, removed a stack of posters, glanced up at Dell.

"I haven't seen any, but you know how that is. We get behind on anything, it's checking those posters all the time."

"Let's take a fast look, then." He indicated the empty chair across from his desk. "Will not take but a minute, and I will know who to look for."

Dell had no desire to look at the crude drawings, but he could see from the expression on Julio's face it would be wise for him to comply. So, he dragged the chair closer, lowered himself into it and began to look at the bad men on sheet after sheet of yellowed paper.

Wanted for murder. Wanted for assault. Wanted for perverted acts. Robbery. Thievery. On and on, over and over — so much crime. So much depravity. After a while he turned away.

"Enough. They aren't there. Somewhere

there is a mother holding the body of her dead child, and that's all that matters. I'm not going after these boys, and I wish no one else would. Because one more of them will die with every sighting. Just leave it for now. I have to go back to Carlton."

Julio glanced out the window. "Going at night?"

"Curly knows the way." He held out his hand.

The Apache had learned most of the ways of the white world and shook hands with him. "Take care, my friend. If I can do anything, please let me know. Your horse is outside."

"Thank you." Dell left before the emotions boiling in him burst forth again. He had a long dark trail on which to vent them in private

Because she'd lost her Stetson to those rowdy boys, her blond hair hung past her shoulders. After brushing the tangled locks and cleaning up, Rose went down the street and pushed through the swinging doors at the Lightning Strike Saloon. Now she'd been in her share of saloons and knew what to expect. Sort of.

One by one, each man in the saloon turned to stare at her. At the badge pinned prominently above the slope of her breast. Probably hadn't heard Carlton had a woman sheriff, since most of them were ramblers. Well, they were soon to find out more than that about her.

The first challenger, a cowboy no taller than her shoulder, reared back as if shocked.

"Hey, lookee here. We either got us a fellow with purty hair or someone's slipped a lady in britches in on us. Is this a joke or what?" He directed the question directly at Rose.

A round of hearty laughter followed from nearby cowboys who overheard him.

She patted him on the back. "Well, lookee here, we either got us a four-year-old all dressed up like his daddy or a dwarf has run away from the circus."

"She's got you there, Sam." He tilted back a battered, sweat-stained Plainsman and held up a frothy beer. "Join me, little lady. Anyone who gets one in on Sam there deserves a drink."

"I'll have a whisky with that if you don't mind."

"Whoa, a woman after my own heart. She wears britches and drinks a man's drink." He turned to the bartender. "Bring the little lady here a whisky and a beer."

She stepped up close to him. "I thank you,

but if you call me 'little lady' again, you're gonna be wearing that there beer you're holding. Name's Rose Parsons."

Those taking in the action roared.

"*Sheriff* Rose Parsons." Her voice bounced over the dying laughter.

Her benefactor handed her the whisky, waited while she slugged it down then gave her the beer which she took a few swallows of and wiped her mouth on the sleeve of her shirt.

"What can we do for you, Sheriff Rose Parsons? None of us wanted by the law, nor fixin to be that I can tell. Name's Matthew Crispin, and I'm pleased to say, I never met me so pretty a sheriff or a lady sheriff."

"I've got a proposition for one of you who can take me up on it. I know a lot of you are waiting for a herd to herd, so to speak."

Grumbles went through the crowd, complaints galore as if she were mocking them. Matthew held up a hand. "Let's wait to hear what the lady has to offer."

"Anyone of you willing to pin on a star and serve as sheriff of Legend County, just till the election when someone can then honestly run for the office? Why I'll promise you a star right here in this place, right now." Total silence. Some looked astonished, others shocked. After a long moment, discussions broke out in groups all over the bar.

Well, at least she'd stirred up something, be it good or bad, it certainly wasn't indifferent. And the word would get out.

She drank her beer, nudged her way to the bar next to Matthew and held it up to the bartender for a refill.

He watched her take a sip. "Tell me about this job you're giving away. I didn't know that's the way it worked. I mean, I thought a fellow — er — anyone had to at least take a test to see if he — er — she knew which end of a gun worked best against the bad men."

"Yeah, you just gonna pick one?" Sam asked from behind her shoulder.

She swallowed, cleared her throat. "Well, you do have to qualify."

"Ah, you all heard that. Qualify. What did you have to do to qualify? Wear britches?"

By then everyone with the exception of a table of poker players was paying attention to the conversation. Must've been fifteen or twenty men in there. If she couldn't get one out of this bunch to take her job so she could ride on, then she'd lost her powers of persuasion.

Sam prodded her. "You didn't answer Matthew's question."

"Which was?"

"Qualify? What? Do we have to shoot somebody to prove we can? Show we can ride a horse?" He pointed at her. "Look like you do in britches?"

"Ain't none of us got a chance if that's the case." This, from the fellow next to Matthew.

Everyone roared and half of them ordered another beer. She ought to ask the owner for a percentage for keeping these old boys bellied up to the bar drinking.

"Well, it's time to get serious. If you're interested in the job it pays forty dollars and found a month."

"What's 'and found' consist of?" Sam asked. "How many dead outlaws we drag in?"

"Well, not exactly. One of your duties is to make sure wild dogs are contained. You get paid for each one you get rid of. You — uh — bring in their ears."

"Holy shit." Someone way down the bar let his opinion be known. "I thought we would be strutting around with a star and a gun making folks behave and the like. Not killing innocent dogs."

Uh-oh, she'd approached this a bit wrong. Some men would rather kill a man any day as kill a dog. "There are other things to do to earn found. But let me ask you, how many are earning forty a month?"

It was quiet while they thought about it. Then a sour voice grumbled. "Would be . . . if we was still herding cattle."

"And working harder for it, I'll bet. I ride around the county checking things out. When called upon I run down some yahoo who shot up a saloon like this one or started a fight in a saloon like this one or stole a horse and ended up with it tied out front of a saloon like this one."

They all groaned.

"Oh, you don't believe me?"

Sam pecked on her shoulder. "Where do I sign up?"

Not exactly the one she would've picked, but maybe the town council would agree to take him on. She could ask him some of the questions they would ask, or she could wait till they met to find out he couldn't qualify. Right now, though, she'd take what she could get.

"Okay, Sam, I'll give you a test, and if you pass it, you can appear before members of the town council to finish qualifying. Okay?"

He looked all around, stuck out his chest. "Ask away."

"In front of all these people?"

"Well, if you'd rather we go to one of the

private rooms, I'd be glad to show you my — uh — other qualifications."

"Oh, funny, Sam. Have you ever been arrested?"

"You mean put in jail?"

"Yep."

"Well, who ain't? Ask any man in here, he'll say yes for some little ole thing that don't really matter."

"Are you saying yes, Sam?"

He nodded. "But it was only for getting drunk and pissing on the corner of the new brick bank in Thomas City. McElroy is sure proud of that place."

"Anything else. Stole a horse, started a fight in public, anything like that?"

He scratched his chin. "Can't say that I have."

"Well, then, can you shoot a gun and hit what you aim at?"

"I reckon I'm pretty fair at it."

"Come on over to the sheriff's office tomorrow and fill out a paper for me to give to the mayor, and he'll be in touch with you. Do you live in Legend County?"

"I can if I need to."

"You'll need to."

He wouldn't be her choice, but at least he was someone. "Anyone else interested in the job?"

Hard to believe no one else showed an interest in a paying job, considering most of them were out of work cowboys. But at least she had one. Things didn't look too good.

Wonder if that man who showed up at Doc's shot in the arm might want the job? A little flesh wound like he had would heal in a few days. Course, he might've been shot in a gunfight with the law. Why hadn't she thought to ask him? Probably because he was bleeding and unconscious at the time. She was sure getting desperate. She bid them all goodbye, thanked them for listening and went back out on the street. Wonder if Dell had ever come back. A lamp still burned in the sheriff's office, so the town marshal must have returned. He should know about Dell.

Carlton was shut down for the night except for the saloons. The two on the other end of town emitted some piano music and occasional laughter. Her town was in good shape, so she went directly to the sheriff's office. Inside she found her friend Sheriff Dell Hoffman sitting in a cell.

"Hey, when'd you get back? Hope those boys didn't give you too much trouble. Send them on their way?"

"Not exactly." He told her what had happened, his voice hitching once in a while.

"Aw, dang, I'm sorry to hear that. What's going to happen now?"

He shrugged. "Not sure yet. I've got to report the shooting to the judge when he makes his rounds. He'll decide if I still have a job and whether I'm going to trial or not."

"The boy tried to kill you."

"And I'm the only witness save for his brothers."

"Well, surely your word against those little savages is good enough."

He studied the floor between his boots for a spell. "I'm not sure I done right, though. He was a child."

"They were all grown, the youngest sixteen. That's not exactly children. I won't let this happen to you, Dell. I'm a witness to their actions toward me. That should be enough."

"Right now, I'm not sure I want you to."

"You're in shock. Not thinking straight. You need to go on home. You've got Guinn to think about."

"After what happened to our Teddy, I'm not sure how she'll feel about me killing that kid."

"Teddy died of whooping cough. He was a baby. There's no comparison. Come on, Dell, why don't you lay down and try to get some sleep? You'll feel more like discussing it rationally in the morning."

"Rationally?" He came to his feet, face turning red. "There's nothing rational about this."

She went to him. "Don't do this to yourself. You're a good man."

After some coaxing she got him to lie down, and the next time she looked in on him he was asleep. Something had to be done to convince him he hadn't done wrong. Usually she kept her nose out of other people's business, but this time she couldn't. She left a note on her desk for him or anyone else who came looking, walked down to the livery where she saddled Cimarron, and rode off toward Thomas City. Guinn would return with her, no doubt in her mind about that. And she could convince him that he needed to defend himself against any charges coming out of this matter. Rose didn't expect any because she would testify as to the boys' actions and treatment of her.

Since she was temporary as Carlton's sheriff, she'd taken a room in Mrs. Banks' rooming house on the outskirts of town. Widow Banks let rooms for an income since her husband Herman had died of the ague last winter. Only one other person stayed there currently, a traveling tinsmith peddler whose wagon was at the smithies for repairs. Rose didn't like the way he stared at her at the breakfast table, so, afraid she might shoot him, she took her meals down at the Brand Iron Café.

This day though, she would have dinner with Guinn, and when she rode up into the yard, the aroma of baking bread spread over her like a comforting breeze. Guinn must've heard her coming for she stood on the porch, one hand shading her eyes from the bright sun. Bet she thought the horse carried Dell.

The woman's face fell when she saw Rose, who dismounted right quick, knowing exactly what Guinn thought.

"Don't worry, ma'am. Dell's fine. He had to stay in Carlton, and so I came by to talk to you about something you can help him — us — with. We've met. My name is Rose Parsons."

Brushing back a stray lock of red hair, Guinn smiled wide. Clapped her hands. "Oh, thank heavens. I knew who you were and thought the worst. That something had happened to that man. I'll swear he gets into a lot of trouble, and it worries me to death. Get down, Rose, and come on in. We'll have something to eat."

Rose grinned right back at her, knowing

how she must feel. Always waiting for someone to come by and tell her Dell had been shot. "I'd be happy to, we need to talk."

With bowls of fragrant stew and a steaming loaf of bread between them, Rose tucked a napkin into her shirt front and took a sip of buttermilk.

"So what is it we need to talk about, Rose?"

Briefly, she told her what had happened with the four boys and how Dell was taking it. "Normally I would've let him tell you about it, but he insisted on staying there in the jail till the county judge, who is due tomorrow, comes through. He thinks he should pay for shooting that boy, even though he would've been shot himself if he hadn't. I couldn't talk him out of it but was sure you could. I hoped you would go back with me."

Before Guinn could reply, the sound of horses arriving in a big hurry brought them both out of their chairs. Rose pushed through the screen door first to face two scruffy men, armed with rifles, and just behind them the oldest of the boys who had mistreated her.

She pulled her gun too late. Gunfire, followed by a burning that slammed into her, knocked her down. For an instant before she passed out, a shrill scream and one of the men cursing filled the air. Then, only darkness.

When she came to, everyone was gone, including Guinn.

Four

"Sheriff, sheriff, you gotta come, there's one heck of a fight downto—"

Dell leaped to his feet, dragged from a deep sleep, to see an excited face peering at him through jail cell bars. "What? Who?"

"You ain't the sheriff?"

Confused, Dell looked around at the strange cell and office. "No, I mean, yes. I am a sheriff, just not the right one. Isn't Sheriff Parsons here anywhere?"

"Ain't seen her, but someone needs to find her and quick. Two men down at the Lightning Strike are tearing up the place fighting. It's getting fierce."

Dell grabbed his hat and gun belt from a hook on the wall. "I'm sheriff in Saddler County. I'll go with you, see what's up."

He hurried along behind the running man arriving just in time to see a flailing body come flying through the swinging doors of the saloon and land with a thud. Another followed right behind him and still another. All three piled in a heap halfway off the boardwalk. One leaped up immediately and went to work hammering on another. The third lay still, blood all over his face.

A group crowded outside, cramming themselves through the door, shouting and shaking their fists in the air. It was one heck of a noisy melee. Dell tried his own hollering but couldn't be heard, so he fired a shot into the air. That got their attention.

Though they quieted some, the one doing the hammering kept it up. Finally, the bouncer from the saloon staggered out and helped Dell pull them apart. One was a giant of a man, but, strangely, he'd been taking the beating off the other, maybe half his size. Dell holstered his gun and took him by the collar. He continued to swing his fists but wound down. The big one lay in the dirt groaning. Dell's prisoner lunged toward his inert opponent, trying to kick him. The other remained out for the count. The bouncer's bald head was covered with blood.

Dell got up in his prisoner's face. "Want me to clock you one, mister?"

"Nope. I want to do that to *him.*"

"What's the problem?"

The smaller guy spit in the direction of

the one on the ground. The other one crawled away, obviously having had enough.

Dell couldn't help but grin. This little feller whipping up on two men bigger than himself, plus doing his best to put down the bouncer, was sort of funny. He held the guy so his feet were off the ground. "You're quite the tiger, aren't you? Settle down, they're both good and whipped. Who started this?"

"I reckon I did."

"What's your name?"

"Sam, and I was just talking about getting the job of sheriff and how if a girl could do it, I could, when they started calling me shorty and little britches and peewee, so I lit into them. Ain't nobody gonna get away with calling me peewee, I don't care how big they are. My pee ain't wee, you get what I mean? Besides, she done told me to come over to the sheriff's office and fill out papers to be sheriff."

Dell chuckled. "Looks like you might qualify. Where'd you see Rose?"

He looked around right quick. "When is it now?"

"Looks like night to me."

"Well, it was this night then. She come into the saloon right soon after we come in for drinks, and that was. . . ." He studied the bouncer, who stood aside supporting the half-conscious target of his fight. " 'Bout eight or so, then she took off. Figured she was going back to the jail house."

"She did. I saw her before I went to sleep. What time is it now?"

One of the men in the crowd drew out his pocket watch, held it up to the lamplight coming through the bar window. "Looks like about eleven. Holy crow, I'd better get home, or the little woman will have my head on a plate."

Where in thunder could Rose be? She should be watching over her town instead of out somewhere no one knew where, galivanting around. "Anyone know if the sheriff was called away for something?"

No one spoke up except Sam who tried to wiggle out of Dell's grip. "She told me flat out to come to the sheriff's office and fill out a paper so I could be sheriff."

Dell turned the small, struggling man loose. "Well, from the looks of things here, you'll be locked up in a cell, and you can wait for her there."

"Aw, sheriff, it was self-defense. You heard what they called me. No man would stand for that." Sam wiped his bloody fist with a bandana.

"A good sheriff would handle it better

than beating the shit out of everyone. Come on with me, or do I have to hogtie you?"

Frowning, Sam agreed. "But least you could do is put them in jail too." He indicated his two victims, one who finally had come to enough to sit on the steps holding his head in both hands and groaning.

Dell eyed the banty of a man. He could use some help, and this man was just the one to lend a hand.

"Okay, Sam. Help me get these two gentlemen on their feet and to the jail. I'll need someone to stay there till I get back. You do it, and that'll tell me if you're sheriff material or not."

"You bet." He went to the one on the steps, grabbed him by the arm. "On your feet, or do I have to help you?"

The guy obeyed without a word.

"The rest of you go on about your business and no more fighting tonight."

The man had some idea how to keep order, anyway. Dell led the way back to the jail with his prisoner. Behind him footsteps followed. He hated to leave these three there, but he had to get back to Thomas City. Guinn would be worried by now, not hearing from him. Rose would have to handle whatever business she had related to Legend County and Carlton. It was her job, and she was probably running down some yahoo. Too bad this place couldn't do better with hiring deputies who could be relied upon to lend a hand. It was a good-sized county with plenty of owlhoots who couldn't behave.

If he left now, he could be home by dawn and have breakfast with his wife. Inside, he gave Sam instructions to hold the two until morning, then fine them each six-bits for disturbing the peace and send them home. Sure, Rose would return shortly. Sam could handle things.

"They don't pay the fine, put them to work cleaning out the cells and the outhouse to work it off. Don't let them get away with anything. Can you do that?"

"Yes, sir, I can. Do I need a badge?"

The man looked so hopeful, Dell hunted through a drawer, found a deputy's star, and pinned it to Sam's chest. "I hereby declare you officially a temporary deputy of Legend County. When Rose shows up, you explain things to her, will you?"

"Yes sir, I can handle this."

"I know you can, Sam — uh — what's your last name?"

"Sam Runkle."

Dell stuck out his hand. "Okay, Deputy Runkle, take care of your town till Sheriff

Parsons returns."

"That I will. And after, too, I hope."

On his way down the street to pick up Curly, a fire in the blacksmith shop detoured him. Chester Reed, a barrel-chested man greeted him warmly.

"Working late, aren't you?"

"Had this job to finish. Folks need their wagon back. Broken wheel. Cooler working at night anyway."

"Sure is, it's been a hot one today. Listen, Chester, would you sort of keep an eye out for any trouble-makers in town? Sheriff Parsons appears to be away on business, and I need to get back to Thomas City. I've left Sam Runkle as a deputy, but if you see he needs a hand, could you help him?"

The bald man grinned, teeth showing white in a face black from smoke. "Be glad to, Sheriff. Hope everything's okay."

"Oh, I think so. It'll be better when the judge can set up an election for a new sheriff and deputy here. This town's been too long without the law."

"It will indeed."

"I've got to get on home. You take care."

"Sure will, you, too."

Dell lifted a hand and headed for the livery.

It would be morning before he got back

home if he rode steady. Sure would be good to sit down with Guinn to a tasty breakfast. Two or three times he nodded off in the saddle, only to awaken to a start when Curly broke stride for a rough patch on the road. At last, the slight uphill climb to the house, which he could see as a shadow in the glow from the eastern sky.

Guinn would be up soon to milk the cow, gather the eggs, and feed the chickens before starting breakfast. Sometimes he was ashamed because she worked harder on the place than he did on his job. But she always said she enjoyed it, and besides, what would she do without some chores to keep her hands busy? Idle hands and all, she'd say.

He rode on to the barn, which they'd only built last year when she said she wanted a milk cow. It made things easier for him, too, keeping Curly there instead of down at the livery. Hanging the saddle and bridle in the tack room, he gave Curly a measure of grain and some hay. The cow stood in her stall, looked at him with wide eyes and mooed loudly. He knelt beside her, touched her bag. She hadn't been milked yet. Was Guinn sick? He hurried to the house. She never overslept.

Strange he couldn't smell bread baking. Maybe she'd made enough yesterday to do them today. Going in the back door he stopped in his tracks. No heat from the cook stove.

What was going on?

What sounded like a low moan came from out front. He ran through the house, checking the front room as he went. Nothing.

Again the moan. Outside, on the porch maybe.

Shoving open the door he headed to the edge of the porch and almost stumbled over Rose, lying in a heap as if she'd tried to climb. Blood pooled around her head and had dripped off the step. She moaned again, this time moving a bit. He dropped down beside her, turned her gently till he could see where she was hurt.

A head wound had bled profusely. Her eyes rolled, and she opened them, tried to speak but couldn't.

"What's happened, Rose? Where's Guinn? Where's my wife?" He wanted to shake her, make her tell him what he needed to know, but she was injured. Heart beating till he almost choked, he checked her over, found no other wound save the head and so struggled till he could pick her up and take her inside where he laid her on the bed in the small front bedroom. What was once their son Teddy's room.

Thinking of the child and his death, he swallowed a knot.

But his Guinn. "Good God, what happened here?" He could barely contain his desire to shout, make her tell him where Guinn was. Someone must've taken her, but why and who and when?

"Water, could I have some water, please?"

Her weak request shamed him, and he ran to the kitchen, poured her a glass, then filled the wash pan with several dippers of cool water, tossed in a washcloth and carried everything back to her.

She was propped on her elbow, and he held the glass to her lips. When she drank her fill, he set it aside. "Lay back down, Rose."

She obeyed, and he gently washed her face, then located the head wound and patted the cloth onto it before inspecting it. The gash was no longer bleeding, but it needed care that he couldn't give. First, though, he had to know what had gone on here. She was alert, and so he sat on the edge of the bed and took her hand.

"Rose, what happened? Where's Guinn? Is she . . . is she alive?"

She nodded. "I don't know. She was alive when they left."

"They? They who?"

"Two men, and they had one of those boys with them." She barely got the words out before closing her eyes. She'd passed out again.

Rather than loading her up to take to Doc, he ran out and down the street to the upstairs office where he found him tending to a man on one of the three beds in the small clinic.

"Doc, you gotta come quick. It's Rose and Guinn. Hurry."

The whiskered man looked up, then back at his patient. "Mom," he shouted. "Could you come in here and care for Miz Murray for a minute."

Dell stood on one foot then the other till Doc's wife hurried in. She took a few low instructions from Doc before Doc joined him.

"Okay, let's go. Tell me what it is on the way." He grabbed his black bag and followed Dell, clambering down the steps and along the boardwalk.

Panting along, he asked, "Is it a gunshot wound?"

"No, she got hit hard on the head."

"Which one? Rose or Guinn?"

"Rose. Guinn is gone. Someone's took her right out of my own house while I was off chasing phantoms."

They reached the porch, and instead of climbing the steps, Dell stopped. "I'm going to saddle up Curly and go find my Guinn. Rose is in the front bedroom. You take good care of her, and I'll be back soon as I can find my wife."

He didn't wait for a reply but ran to the barn. Cast a fast glance at the suffering cow. "Sorry old girl, I'll send someone over to milk you." He finished saddling Curly as he spoke to the cow, then was mounted and riding off. His neighbor down the road would milk the cow, and he stopped and made arrangements, then was off again.

First thing was find those boys, and the last place he'd seen them was south of Carlton. So he rode at a full gallop till Curly started chuffing then slowed to a walk. Wouldn't do to kill his horse and be afoot. It was midafternoon when he reached the spot Rose had described. An Indian message tree was bent in growth to point out a hidden stream nearby. The earth was churned up where the boys had roped and tied her. Because the four of them had left good tracks off the beaten path and through the woods, he followed easily. He slow-tracked their horses through the woods and to a farmhouse in a meadow, about three miles from the main trail between Carlton and Hawkins Post.

He rode toward it slowly, arms spread to each side in a peaceful gesture. It did no good. Two bullets cut the dust at Curly's feet. Two more severed a small limb from an overhanging tree branch. Heavy with leaves it fell across the horse's rump. He spooked, leaped to one side. Kicking loose from the stirrups Dell dismounted and dived into the nearby bushes.

Five

A fuzzy face peered down at Rose. *Get away from me. Away.* She tried to raise her fist. Nothing. What was she doing lying on her back with a walloping headache? Turning to see where she was, and someone hit her with a hammer. Blackness filled with flying stars shut out the light.

"Rose? Rose girl, open your eyes." A voice, wavering, unclear.

Stop. Leave me alone. Had she said the words or thought them? Hard to tell. A ringing bell replaced the stars. Now she had to cover her ears.

"It's me, Doc Kelton. Lay still, Miss Rose. You could cause more damage moving about."

More damage, and she'd go crazy. His image cleared up a bit. It was Doc. Not the men who'd done this. She struggled to speak to him, but he just kept telling her what to do.

"You've been hit in the head, and you need to be still, or it may hurt worse. Don't struggle. I'm a doctor trying to see to you."

Stop saying that. I know who you are. But what happened? Why couldn't she say anything? *Ask* him anything?

Silent, she continued to stare at him.

Doc cleaned the head wound, which hurt like the very devil. To make up for it he placed a cool cloth on her forehead. Then he went to talking to her some more.

"I want you to stay very still for a time to make sure you don't stir that wound into something worse." He took her hand. "Can you tell me what happened? Who did this to you? Just don't get excited."

"Where's Guinn?" Finally, she was able to say something clearly.

"Dell's gone to search for her. Do you remember who did this to you?"

"Yes."

"You do? Why? Do you know?"

In her excitement to tell him what happened she tried to rise, but Doc held her down. "Careful now. Just take it easy and tell me."

"The boys who took me." Slowly the words rolled off her lips.

"It was them?"

"No, no. One of them and two men.

Maybe the dad and uncle?" She shuddered and closed her eyes.

"Okay, take it easy now. Just lie there a moment, and if you think of something, why then tell me but slow and without tossing around."

In spite of what he said, she struggled to sit, held her swimming head in both hands. "You've got to tell Dell. I just remembered. They took Guinn."

"I'll go get someone to catch up to him and tell him. Will you be all right here? Stay in bed. I'll send someone up here to stay with you. Promise me you'll stay right where you are till she gets here."

"I will, I promise. Go. Find Dell so he knows what happened."

The screen door slammed. Another banging roused her, and she opened her eyes. A tree limb, swaying in the wind hitting the house and the window.

So tired. Her head ached so bad. She closed her eyes, and the next time she opened them, the sun had slipped all the way west and rested on the horizon, turning the sky a blazing orange with streaks of purple slashed across it. No one had come to stay with her. Guess Doc couldn't find anyone, or something came up.

Gingerly she pulled her knees up, then slid

her feet across the bed and off onto the floor. A bit dizzy but not bad. She took a few deep breaths and sat all the way, leaning back on both hands. Still the same. Getting to her feet would no doubt be the hardest, and if she fell, it would be further to the floor. So, she sat there a while, thinking of Dell and Guinn and what might be happening to them. Then, without further thought, she pushed herself upright and took hold of the chair back near the bed.

Hmm, not too bad.

All of a sudden the room took off in wide circles, and she went in smaller circles. Her stomach found another way to go and threatened to turn loose its contents. Tears poured down her cheeks, and she dropped to the bed to keep from throwing up. Where was everyone? Why hadn't Doc sent someone up here? She needed to go after Dell, help him find Guinn.

Someone with a kind voice came into the room. "Oh, you darling girl, lie still now. Name's Emma Lou Cartwright. Doc sent me up to sit with you. I've been in the kitchen cooking you some soup. Didn't want to waken you."

At last Rose could see clearly, and she checked out the small room, walls painted blue, curtains for a child. Oh, yes. Poor little

Teddy's room. Dell and Guinn's child. A lamp on the bedside table cast a golden glow. The woman was plump and pretty, her silver hair done up in a bun. She wore a green dress with white trim.

"Have they found Dell or Guinn?"

"I haven't heard anything. You stay right like you are, and I'll bring you a bowl of chicken soup."

Despite all the worry, she was hungry, and the soup sure smelled good. The woman came back carrying a tray with a steaming bowl, a glass of milk, a bowl of butter, and a chunk of bread lay on a napkin.

"Sorry to be so late. Had to milk that poor old cow, she was fit to bust and calling out. So, this is fresh, and Guinn left bread in the warming oven." She moved the lamp a bit and placed the tray on the table.

Rose scooted to the edge of the bed, put her feet on the floor and sipped some of the milk. It was warm and creamy, and she drank it all, held up the glass. "Could I have more, please?"

She moved closer to the food, spooned out some soup and blew on it before placing it in her mouth. So good. Not able to remember when she last ate, she kept at the soup till Emma returned with more milk.

"Well, it looks like you're feeling better.

I'll get you some more, if you'd like."

Buttering the bread, Rose nodded, dropped the bread, and grabbed her head. It felt like something hard rolled around up there banging from one side to the other.

Emma bustled in with more soup. "Are you all right? You look pained."

"Head still hurts some, but I'm fine." To prove it, she took the bowl and made short work of it.

She finished off the milk and buttered bread, wiped her mouth and nose, only feeling a bit dizzy.

Emma took her arm. "You should remain in bed. Doc said so."

"Do you know where my horse is?"

Emma turned firm. "I do not, and I'm supposed to keep you here till Doc says you can leave. So please do sit down before you fall down."

"Don't be silly, I'm fine. I need to go help them look for Guinn. No telling what those nasty men are doing to her."

Emma gripped her arm, and about the time she did, Rose's knees gave out, and her head swam. Emma guided her onto the mattress, put her feet up, and covered her with a sheet. "You just lie right here. I'll be in the other room if you need anything."

Emma left with the lamp and shut the

door. The bedroom darkened. Rose did her best to rise, but the whirling around her said different, and she gave in to it.

Total darkness surrounded her when she opened her eyes. What happened? Where was she? For no reason she could think of, tears flowed. It must have been a bad day.

Hidden in the bushes, Dell waited for more shots but none came. Off in the distance a woman shouted. "You boys stop that shooting and git to the house. Dinner is ready, and your pa is hungry."

Well, at least now he had a chance to approach and look around, see if they were holding Guinn here. If the boys' pa took her, and he was there, then she couldn't be far away. There were two men, though, and one could have her somewhere else. Or maybe Rose was wrong, and it was someone else who took Guinn, but he had to go on what he believed, at least for now.

Being a lawman was sometimes purely hard. But all the clues were with him, and he had to take a chance they had Guinn till it was proven different. Three young men and two grown men plus a woman he couldn't write off could easily outgun him. Rose was a woman, and he wouldn't want to go against her, so he had to count them all in figuring on a plan. To come out alive with his wife, he had to get the drop on them in one room, then convince them to tell him where his wife was. No easy task.

He checked his gun. If he had to kill once more to get Guinn, he would but face it. He'd killed one of those boys and didn't want to do it again. Didn't like the way it made him feel. Shooting grown men who had a gun pointed at him was one thing, but that was another. His heart, his soul, neither liked it at all. But Guinn. Dear God, he couldn't let them harm that sweet woman, the only woman he'd ever loved or ever would. He knew that with a certainty. God forgive him he would kill for her.

There was plenty of ammunition in his belt, the six-shooter was loaded, but they'd never give him time to reload.

Well, shit, Dell. Stop thinking and get in there and take care of business.

Halfway to the house, using what little growth there was in the yard to hide behind, he could hear them carrying on a conversation, silverware clinking as they ate. Laughter. How could they possibly laugh with what they had done, what they were fixing to do? What kind of people were they?

A bush heavy with fragrant white blooms grew right next to the back porch steps, giving him a hiding place near the back door which had a screen. From there, he stared into the kitchen at the table they were gathered around. One man sat at the head, the other plus one boy had their back to him, two boys faced him, and the woman was opposite the head. His best spot would be behind her, gun to her head. That'd put him facing the men and boys. But he had to cross half the kitchen to do that.

Well, then, stop thinking and go. Surprise them. Damn screen, he had to get it open first. And fast. Do it, damn it. Just do it.

And he did. Opened the screen, took two long steps around the table, gun pointed at the woman all the time. Finally, behind her, one hand under her chin, the other holding the barrel of the six-shooter at her head.

One of the men came partway to his feet, the woman screamed, the other man just stared open mouthed. The boys dropped their silverware and gaped. Then the biggest one halfway stood, looked toward the head of the table.

"Pa? He killed Pete."

Face gone hard, Pa waved a hand at him. "Sit down, boy. We'll see what he wants."

"What I want is my wife. You and one of your boys grabbed her last night, and all I want is her back. No tricks or nothing else."

The man barked a laugh. "We ain't took yore wife. What makes you think that?"

Dell squeezed the woman's chin hard till she howled with pain. "No talking about it, or I take this one, and you won't see her again. Understand?"

"Pa, I can go —" One of the boys half rose.

"Shut up. Now. I don't think he means it."

Dell tilted her head back, aimed the gun, and shot the man next to him in the shoulder, so fast no one moved. He held up the gun then aimed it at her head. "By my calculations there are still enough bullets in here to take care of the rest of you. One by one, till I get my wife in this room unharmed. And sometimes my aim is off just enough to kill. Got that?"

The younger boy shoved his chair back, darted a look in the direction of the man at the head of the table, the one they called Pa, and ran from the room out the back door.

"Get yourself back here, Chip." Pa yelled that.

There was no reply. For a moment, the room was so quiet only their breathing could be heard. Then the other man said under his breath, "Son of a bitch."

Dell told them to let the boy go. Up to that point, he hadn't identified himself as the sheriff of Saddler County, and obviously they didn't know. He'd thought it best not to say so, either. Now, he didn't.

"That boy comes back in here with my wife, then I'm taking you and your other two boys to jail. Him I'm leaving here with his mother in the hopes he sees how he helped hisself by righting a wrong."

He must've turned his look away from the other man for an instant, for he jumped across the corner of the table between them just far enough to jostle Dell's gun arm, then slid on to take him to the floor. The gun went off, and all was again silent. Then the woman went to her knees and screamed "Carl" and threw herself on the man.

Dell came out from under the two but not in time to stop Pa who ran out the door, maybe with the intent to stop the kid bringing Guinn in. Dell went right behind him, gun still in one hand. Was he going to have to shoot the lot of them? So far he'd shot one twice, and he was sure the last bullet was fatal. He didn't have time to check but ran instead close behind Pa. At the back of the house was a shed, about half falling down. Pa hit the door hard, Dell right behind him. Nothing in there but tools and junk, bags of stuff.

"What the hell?" Pa turned a complete circle.

Dell knocked him down, grabbed the front of his shirt. "Where is she?"

"I–I don't know. She was here. Right here."

"Where would he take her?"

"I have no idea."

Dell pointed his gun. "For two cents I'd just shoot you right now. What's the matter with you? Teaching your boys like this after you already lost one of them to such actions."

"You killed my boy, damn you. You think I'm not going to get back at you somehow?"

Dell just shook his head. That this man could not see that the boy's actions brought about his death, and him teaching the other three it was okay, would one day do the same for them. He was damned sorry he had to shoot that kid — would never get over it, in fact. But this man was as much to blame as anyone.

With anger and fear in his heart, Dell holstered his gun and tied the man to a corner post in the shed, then went in search of the boy and Guinn. They had to be nearby. He could just hope the boy had some good left over after the teachings of his pa so he wouldn't kill her.

Outside, the afternoon sun blinded him while he scanned his surroundings. Where could that boy be? Movement down toward the barn behind a pile of equipment. Dell took off down a slight slope. Cows grazing off to one side of the ramshackle building all chewed their cud and stared in that direction. Now cows are curious animals, so something was going on down there. He jerked his gun back out of its holster and skidded around a rusty plow leaning against a fence post. There, crouched behind some other pieces of farm equipment, was the kid. Alone.

Heels planted in the dirt, Dell came to a halt. "Where is she?"

The boy shrugged, then grinned, and it was the creepiest thing Dell had ever seen. Pure evil in a smile is a terrible thing to see. One day he would get full pay for his actions. Racing past him, Dell went into the big old barn.

Sunlight cut the darkness in bars that slipped in through cracks between the gray boards that had given up in their effort to hold up the roof. It sagged in the center like its back was broken. In one shadowy corner, a room beckoned. He jerked open the door, for a moment could scarcely see through the gloom.

"Dell?"

He fell on his knees near the weak plea. "Yes, yes. It's me." He crawled to the sound of her sobs, hands touching her dress ballooned out around her crouching figure. Unable to make out her face at all, he felt up her legs to her body, then her shoulders. Her arms were bent behind her, probably tied.

"You okay, Guinn. Okay?" Fingers walked through tears over her face, into her hair. Tangled, hanging loose but no blood there.

"I'm tied, the ropes are cutting me. Get me loose, please, Dell."

He dug out his pocketknife, proud that he kept it sharp as a razor. "Can you move? Where I can't see the rope, I'm afraid of cutting you."

She toppled to her stomach and in the dim light coming through one crack her ankles and wrists were tied together behind her back, so tight it must be hurting her bad. The bastards. He wanted to rush out and beat the very life out of them. Instead he found the rope binding feet to hands and cut it first, so she was lying flat. She cried out when it came loose, and he rubbed her shoulders gently. Next, the ropes around her wrists because her arms were bent so far back it had to hurt dreadfully.

He definitely was going back in there and shooting every last one of them. Putting the world out of its misery for having to ever deal with any of them again. There was certainly punishment for such wickedness, some action that would hunt each one of them down and make them pay.

All the while these thoughts went through his head, he worked at freeing his lovely wife, and when he finally cut through the last of the bindings, he turned her over, picked her up, and carried her through the sun-striped old barn and out into the light.

The boy still crouched behind the plow as if paralyzed with fear.

"You, get her some water. Now."

Evidently his voice meant business because the boy ran off and came back with a dipper of cold water.

Dell knelt, and, propping her upright against one raised knee, he held the dipper to her mouth. She drank like one starving for water, and, when the dipper was empty, she licked the outside. His heart went out to her. He wished he had the power to damn these people to hell. Somewhere it existed, and sooner or later it would find them.

She whimpered, leaned her head into his shoulder. This was what he had to do. Care for her, take her home. He couldn't do that and haul them in to justice at the same time. He stared at the boy, whose eyes were wide with fear.

"I'm taking her home. You and your family of animals are to leave Texas. You understand me? When I come back — and I will — there'd better not be any sign of you, or I'll send you *all* to Hell where you belong. You got that?"

The boy nodded so hard his teeth clacked.

Dell picked up his wife, carried her to where Curly waited, and helped her gently into the saddle. He took up the reins and walked off through the woods, following the trail he'd come in on. He never looked back.

Six

Thunder awoke Rose. At least that's what she thought it was. A loud rumbling that faded away to the sound of rain pounding the roof. A roof. Now, where was she? It was hard, waking up in strange places in the dark. Lightning flashed and solved that problem momentarily but did nothing to identify her location. Memory of the day before drifted back like fog trailing in.

If that memory served her right, she should still be at Dell's house where she'd come yesterday. And then the happenings of the day before returned. If in its entirety, then Dell and Guinn hadn't come home yet. They were both still missing. There should be a lamp on the bedside table. Rising, she felt across the top until her fingers touched the glass base. Where there was one, there was usually a way to light it. Matches. Yes, a small holder of them with a striker pad. She brushed one across the pad, lifted the chimney, touched flame to wick, and adjusted it to stop smoking.

A space around her came to life, and she experimented getting upright slowly. When she could stand without falling on her face, she took up the lamp and went through the front room into the kitchen. What next? She turned to check the other bedroom just in case they'd come home without waking her. Her arm hit a pot sitting on the water tank of the stove. The pot hit the floor and bounced noisily before rolling to a stop.

Fright sent her leaping and brought Emma Lou out of the dark bedroom yelling. "Who is it? What's that?"

Rose faced her. Emma squared off as if ready to fight. She stopped. "What are you doing up, Miss Rose?"

"I'm really not sure. I awoke, wondered who might be here and decided to get up and see."

"Well, you and I are here, and with all that clatter, if anyone else was, we'd know it by now."

Before she could say more, a jagged finger of lightning beyond the window tied the sky to the ground, cracked like the world had split, and sent a long roll of thunder that shook the house till dishes rattled in the cupboard. Rose shivered from head to toe.

"My, that was a good one, huh?" Emma reached out to touch Rose. "I'll bet you could use a cup of coffee, or would you rather go back to sleep?"

"Coffee would be nice. Could I build up the fire?"

"If you're up to it. Not dizzy or anything?"

Rose went to the wood box and took out a fistful of kindling. "No, I'm fine. My head is sore, but that's all." She opened the stove, stirred up some coals and laid in the thin shavings of wood. Smoke, then flame trickled, and she fed it with small sticks. By the time she had a fire, Emma had fixed a percolator of water with a basket of grounds.

While it perked, Rose sat across from Emma at the table, toying with a spoon and staring into an empty china cup. "Do you suppose they're okay? Shouldn't we have heard something by now? And, what with this storm, I hope they aren't out in it."

"I do, too. Mister Dell, he'll be fine. He's used to being out in all weather. But Miss Guinn, she's liable to take a cold or pneumonia, out in this."

"Uh-huh. What about you and your husband? Won't he be worried about you not coming home last night?"

"My husband was killed in a cattle drive several years ago. I've got no one at home now." She glanced around the cozy room. "In fact, I'm more pleased to be here with you as to be home alone in this storm."

Not knowing quite how to reply to that, Rose kept her silence. Being alone suited her. She didn't want to have to come up with something to say anyone might want to hear. Whether riding the plains or sitting in a saloon or beside a campfire, alone was best.

But right now, she'd give anything to hear Dell and Guinn come riding up, to know they were safe. Then she could be on her way to hunting down those men who'd come riding out here and visited violence upon her friends. Even if there weren't wanted posters on any of them, she would hunt them down and do what it was she did.

Mean as they were, they deserved that and more.

"Miss Rose?"

Startled out of her thoughts, Rose jumped. "Yes?"

"Would you tell me . . . What's it like to be an unmarried woman doing what you please and all?"

"I . . . uh, but you're almost — you're alone as I am. You said several years ago your husband — well, it's what I like. I've never been any other way, so I have nothing to compare it to. I do what I please when I please as long as the law says I can. What do you do, day to day?"

"I suppose it's what I please, except I always stop and wonder what Earl would think. But that's not what I mean. I mean, what really do you do? Since he died, I've wondered."

"Well, mornings I take a walk if I'm where I can. Just to watch the world come alive with the sun. Then I cook a good breakfast. Eggs, bacon or ham, preserves, butter, bread." She laughed. "I don't bake well, but in most places someone does and sells me a loaf or some rolls. If I'm traveling, I still take the walk or ride Cimarron out across the plains at breakneck speed. Then I'm off looking for my latest prisoner. Sometimes that means sitting in a sheriff's or marshal's office going through all the wanted posters."

Emma's eyes gleamed. "How do you catch them? I mean sneak up on them and bonk them over the head? Maybe ask some man to go with you to help?"

"Lord, no. Not a man's help, seldom ever. Sometimes I have to persuade them with a gun, sometimes with women's wiles."

"Oh, dear. You don't . . . not really?"

Rose laughed. "I'll never tell, Emma."

"Why, Miss Rose."

"You ought to try it sometime, you might like it." It might brighten up what must be a very dull life for this woman, but Rose wouldn't tell her that.

A horse approached, galloping hard. Rose beat Emma to the back door in time to get a glimpse of a rider going into the barn in the lightning.

"Must be Dell, but no one's with him."

"Oh, dear. Suppose he hasn't found Miss Guinn?"

"I can't think he'd quit till he did, but. . . ." Rose could hardly breathe for the fear that grew inside her.

It seemed forever before the rider sloshed through the mud and rain to stomp off his boots at the back door and hustle inside. Dell, and he was alone.

Her fear turned to hatred of those men and what they'd done. She'd hunt them down to the ends of the earth if she had to.

Dell shed his rain gear and Stetson, hung them on hooks and kicked out of his muddy boots.

"I smell coffee."

Emma Lou jumped to her feet, poured him a cup, and set it before him at the table. Rose waited as did the other woman, waited for him to say what had happened. His features, wet with rain, were drawn, but he didn't look like something bad had happened. He just looked weary and in need of sleep.

After taking four or five gulps of the black coffee, he set down the cup. "She's okay. I left her with Doc Payne in Carlton. Didn't want to bring her on horseback in the storm, and it seemed better than waiting around to maybe rent a wagon to bring her home in. I'm going to fetch her soon as the rain lets up."

He drank some more coffee. "I wanted to stay, sit right there with her, but she ordered me home." He grinned. "And you know how stubborn she can be. I didn't want to fight with her after what she's been through."

More coffee, and he eyed Rose. "You okay?"

She nodded, stood, and refilled his cup.

"No headache or anything?"

"No. Dell, tell us what happened." How could he just sit there drinking coffee and not reveal what had gone on? "How'd you find her? What'd you do to those men?"

He emptied the cup and rose, stretched. "After I sleep, Rose. Let me get some sleep, and I'll tell you the whole story." With that, he headed for the bedroom, shut the door, and that was that.

"Dang the man."

Emma chuckled. "You'd probably do the same, little as you like to talk about yourself and your adventures. Oh, I'm so happy Miss Guinn is okay."

"If she was okay, he wouldn't have left her at the doctor's. She'd have ridden home on Curly's back with him or on a rented mount. I know Guinn. She's far from okay. She's just not dying or bad hurt, for which I'm thankful. Still, I can't sit around here waiting to hear. Why couldn't he at least tell us where those men are — if they got away or he shot them or what?"

Without saying so, she hoped in her heart that he'd punished them bad, even shot them dead. But she kept her thoughts to herself. Though she didn't really care what people thought of her, she'd taken a liking to Emma Lou, or at least she felt sorry for her and so wanted her to not think badly of her.

Dell had ridden all the way home regretting that he hadn't kept his word and taken that man and his boys to jail and locked them up in the absence of a sheriff, but Guinn was in such a bad way she needed Doc bad.

So, he'd simply taken her away, leaving his promise to come back and kill them all if they didn't leave Texas and take the wounded one with them. Walking to Carlton in the pouring rain while keeping her in the saddle had exhausted him so, that when he left her with Doc Payne and made the long ride home, he was too tired to tell his story to Rose and Emma Lou.

Sunlight streamed across the bed when he awoke. A belly growling aroma of meat cooking beckoned, and he dressed quickly to join the women in the kitchen. He filled the wash pan with hot water from the reservoir and quickly washed up.

Emma Lou stood over the stove. "Good morning, Mister Hoffman."

He dried his hands and face and regarded her. "Good morning. You been here all day?"

She nodded. "Miss Rose needed someone to look after her, and I got no place I need to go."

"Where is she?"

"In bed. She went back there after you come in with the news that Missus Hoffman was alive. Is she going to be all right? What did the doctor say?"

"Dehydrated, exhausted, sore from being tied up for so long. He said she'll be okay after some rest and good food. I'm going back to bring her home. But I believe I'll have a plate of whatever that is you're cooking. It smells delicious."

"I hope you don't mind, I went to the smokehouse and brought in a ham. I knew you and Missus Hoffman would need a good meal. And Miss Rose, too. There's some potatoes, and I picked green beans from the garden earlier today. I believe it's all ready to eat. I'm going to let Miss Rose sleep. She needs the rest."

He pulled out a chair and sat down while Emma Lou filled a plate from the stove. "That's a good idea. I sure appreciate your staying with her. I wonder if you'd consider remaining a few days with Guinn. I'd be glad to pay you."

He dug into the steaming food. It tasted better than anything he'd had at least since Guinn was taken. Just the thought made his blood boil. He'd be going back to that farm as soon as she was settled. It'd be too bad for anyone who was still there. They'd better be good and gone. In his secret heart, he hoped he could drag them all off to jail. Or maybe that the old man would give him a good reason to wallop him good first. He couldn't abide men who hurt women or kids.

Rose must've heard them talking for she came in rubbing her eyes.

"Let me fix you a plate." Emma Lou began that job without waiting for a reply.

Rose washed her hands and sat in a chair across from Dell. "Mmm, that smells so good. Thank you. Aren't you going to eat anything, Emma?"

"Yes, please do." Dell added his invitation to hers.

Emma fixed herself some food and joined them.

"Now, Dell, tell us what happened."

He did, keeping it short because what that family had done to Guinn made him so angry, he could barely speak in a normal voice.

Rose regarded him closely. "You left them there? Alive?"

"All but one. He drew down on me. Got him in the shoulder. The uncle, I believe. Would you have me kill them all?" For an instant he wished he had.

"I'm surprised you didn't, considering what they did."

"The woman and boys, too?"

She dropped her gaze to fork up some potatoes and beans. "Well, maybe just the old man. But those boys are well on the way to being as bad as he is. I don't know what can be done about them."

"I'm going back tomorrow, and if they're still there, we'll see."

"I'm going with you."

He jerked his head up from taking a bite of ham. "What're you intending on doing?"

"I haven't decided yet. Might depend on what you do. If I find out they're any of them on a poster, you can bet I won't hesitate."

"Rose, you won't knowingly break the law. That I know." He grinned. "At least not in my presence."

"I need to get on back to Carlton. I'm concerned about how Sam's getting along keeping the law there. There's an outlaw over there I want to visit with."

"Uh-oh, guess that means you're hunting bounty again. I think Sam will do just fine. I saw him drag in two of the biggest, meanest owlhoots in town. That little man is a whirlwind."

"Is that right? If he's good as you say, I'm getting the city council to call a special meeting and hire him, then heading west over toward Palo Duro. Maybe pay a call on that old friend. I *do* have a private life, you know."

Dell took another bite, chewed thoroughly, and drank some iced tea Emma had poured for everyone, then went on as if he hadn't heard her last declaration. "In fact, I pinned a deputy's badge on Sam after he said he'd talked to you and was going to be the next sheriff."

"He said what?"

"You heard me. Didn't you tell him that?"

"Well, not exactly. I was putting him off by telling him he had to come to the office and pick up some papers to fill out to become sheriff."

Dell laughed. "Well what he heard was he would become sheriff. Don't worry, he was doing fine when I left, and you can explain things to him 'cause he thinks he's going to be sheriff, and, frankly, I think he might make a good one. Temporarily, that is. Hell, he can't be as bad as that no count deputy who don't show up half the time, and when he does, he's not worth his weight in horse hockey."

"Whew, that's good, 'cause I'm tired as can be of playing a lawman." She ate for a while, then looked up. "So, can I ride on back with you? I'd sort of like to see Guinn before I go on my way."

He arched a brow. "Long as you promise me you won't go on out to that farm and tear up Ned with them people. I'm going to handle this myself, in my own way."

"Okay, I promise. But I'm telling you one thing, folks like that are gonna get their comeuppance, from one source or another. And, if they ever come up on a wanted poster, it'll be from me."

Secretly he hoped she was right, but he'd seen many a bad man wreak havoc and see no retribution. Then he grinned. Course that was if they didn't get on a wanted poster and in Rose Parsons's sights.

He thanked Emma Lou for the delicious meal and rose from the table. "I'm fixin' to leave. If you're going with me, Rose, you'd best get to moving."

She hurried around, then stopped in the middle of the floor. "In all the excitement about Guinn I forgot about Cimarron. Where is he? What did they do with him?"

"He's out in the barn. They must've brought you in on him. I never thought to mention it."

"And that one stole my dadgum Stetson. It was new, too."

"I've got an old one you can have. Might be a tad big for your head, but it'll keep the sun off. Looks like its bearing down out there today."

He went into the bedroom and retrieved the tan hat he'd worn till Guinn bought him the new one for his birthday. He perched it on Rose's head and went to the door.

"Well, come on, girl. We're burning daylight." Suddenly he couldn't wait another minute to be on his way back to Carlton and Guinn. The fear that she had been hurt bad or even killed had taken a big chunk out of him. He hadn't thought he could hurt that bad since Teddy died. If he lost her too, there'd be no reason to go on.

The sky and prairie were washed clean from the storm, puddles of water shimmering in the midday sunlight. A breeze carried the scent of wet, clean earth. Both horses whinnied loudly when they approached the barn as if calling on them to hurry so they could be set free. Rose groaned when she swung her saddle onto Cimarron's back, but he knew better than to offer to help. She'd slap him sideways. He'd never met such an independent woman. Had thought Guinn to be till Rose came along.

Once they were underway, he relaxed in the saddle. No sense in being anxious now. His Guinn was safe with Doc. He couldn't imagine what made men like those who'd taken her and roughed up Rose. She wasn't much of a talker, so they rode in silence most of the way to Carlton, one or the other remarking on something once in a while. The sun lay on the horizon, a brilliant red, as it slipped slowly out of sight, when he spotted the church steeple that marked the edge of the town.

There ought to be people wandering around town, but it was deserted. Not late enough for everyone to be home for the night. No wagons on the street. He peered toward the millinery and saw a closed sign on the door.

"What's going on here?" He glanced at Rose. "I'm going down to Doc's, find out."

"Strange. I'm going on to the sheriff's office."

On his way, a wagon came rattling down the street. The driver, a rancher from off toward Thomas City a ways, stopped next to him. "What's the matter with this here town? I come in to buy some feed, and the store's locked up tight as a drum. Thought maybe he was sick, so I stopped at the mercantile to get some supplies, and it's the same. What the Sam Hill's going on here?"

"I don't know, just got here myself, but I aim to find out."

"I'm going with you. Ain't no telling what's up." The rancher tied his team at a nearby hitching post and leaped down, holding a rifle.

Dell dismounted and tied Curly, too. No, there wasn't any telling. He was nervous and relieved someone was with him. "I'm Sheriff Hoffman from up Thomas City way. My wife's at the doctor's, and that's where I'm headed."

"I'm Lucas Brown. I thought I recognized you."

At the bottom step, Dell drew his six-shooter. "Best we're quiet."

Rifle at the ready, Brown nodded and followed Dell up the steps. At the door they both hesitated before Dell turned the knob and shoved it open while standing to one side.

Inside was gloomy with the evening darkness, but shadows showed that things were flung around the room, papers lay everywhere, and a chair was overturned. In the back room the beds were ripped clean of linens, and someone lay hunched in the corner.

Dell dropped down beside him, took his shoulder. "Doc. Doc. You okay? What happened here?"

The old man groaned and held the side of his face. Lucas Brown came in from another room. "Sheriff. Sheriff. There's a woman in the other room. I think she's dead."

Seven

Rose stepped onto the boardwalk in front of the sheriff's office, shaded her eyes, and peered in. Through the dirty glass the place looked empty. She was going to have to ask someone to clean that window. It sent lazy messages about the local law.

Hand cupped over her Colt, she shoved the door open with her toe and crept inside. What the thunder was going on? Someone should be here. Maybe she'd been right about Sam, and he wasn't ready for this job. Hugging the wall, she made it into the room where cells stood empty and quiet. Two men had been brought in yesterday, according to Dell, so, where were they? Back outside, the empty street didn't bode well for Carlton. Folks should've been hurrying to finish their shopping before heading home for supper. What was going on?

Returning to the office, she checked the gun cabinet. Empty. Time to warn Dell something bad was going on. He'd left to fetch Guinn and take her home. Outside, she grabbed Cimarron's reins but didn't mount. Best to move quietly. So, she led him down the street, peering into stores, already closed, and she presumed locked. It was more important that she find Dell. Right now, anyway. Time for that later, when they decided what to do. At Doc's, she led her horse into the alleyway out of sight of the main street, tied him to the rail of the porch steps, and crept up. No noise from inside, but the door stood wide open. Tip-toeing through the trashed room into the back, she drew up fast.

Dell sat on a cot, a man with a rifle standing behind him. A body on the floor in the corner.

She pulled out her gun. "Okay, you drop that weapon, now."

The man let go the thing like it was hot.

Dell leaped to his feet. "Rose, it's okay, don't shoot. He's with me."

Hard to believe. She looked around the room fast. Held tight to her aim. "Dell, you sure? Who's that dead over there?"

"Rose, put it away. Now. Someone's broke in here, killed Doc Payne and his wife, and took Guinn."

"*Again?* How can that be?"

"That's what we've been discussing. This here's Lucas Brown. He rode into town a while ago and found it like it is now. But he didn't see anything else going on. I don't know where to go from here. But I think I made a big mistake setting those people loose. They must've come right here and done this."

Rose dropped down beside him. "I'm sorry about Guinn and poor Doc and his wife. I didn't know him or her but to see them on the street once in a while. Is the entire town like this?"

"Places I went were locked up." Brown scowled. "Course, I only went to the feed store and the mercantile. Then there's this here place. I'd say, with the evidence we've got — empty streets and boardwalks — everyone in town's disappeared."

"No one's at the sheriff's office, not even the two men you said Sam took in yesterday." She looked at Dell, whose eyes shimmered with tears. What had happened to Guinn? And why? It was crazy.

"I don't think four men could accomplish this, Dell. Either they had a lot of help, or it's a gang looking to take over the entire town."

He shook his head. "If it were that, where are they? Why would they do this then ride out? My Guinn is gone again, and I don't know where to look for her."

She rose, slapped her thighs. "First thing, and I hate to say this, but we need help. We either call in my friends or yours."

"That's as good an idea as any, but your friends walk the line between the law and outlawry."

"That's true. But they're outlaws who do what they do because they don't think some things are exactly fair to poor folks. Not those who go around shooting up stagecoaches and trains or mistreating folks like farmers and ranchers. Those owlhoots I haul in for bounty. I can get us a bunch who are wild and not afraid to stand up for what's right and who will break the law to protect those who are helpless. You can get us some lawmen who, granted though they're tough, won't go all the way when it comes right down to some acts that aren't legal."

Dell jumped to his feet. "As a sheriff, I can't go around breaking the law. But if we have to do it to get Guinn back, then I'll lay down my badge. Now, first, I'm gonna cover the Paynes. Then we need to check out this town. There may be someone here who saw something, or we might find a clue who stole her. Come on."

Lucas took up his gun. "I'm with you on this. I ain't for killing no one, but I ain't for outlaws who take women hostage either."

Dell hurried out ahead of Rose. "This time I'm killing the son of a bitch who hurts her, that's for sure. You got any objections to that then go on home."

Lucas fell in behind Rose. "I'm coming with you."

"Let's check out the stores first. Might be someone hiding out who knows what happened."

With darkness coming on, the deserted street lay in deep shadows. The wind stirred up a few dust devils as if to warn of worse times to come. And the first worse thing was, it was eerily silent, as if death stalked them.

Rose took one side of the street, the two men the other. She was quick with a gun and could handle anything that came up. At least that's what she told Dell when he objected. Then she walked off from the two of them. Men sometimes could be so hardheaded about what a woman could accomplish. Dell should know, but he was so upset over Guinn's absence, he wasn't thinking of much else.

The first store, a leather maker's, presented a locked door, and she hammered on it, called out, then listened for the slightest sound. No sense in breaking glass if no one was there. Any captives could manage to kick the wall or holler. One store after the other, she checked while standing out of the way of a bullet. All the way to the livery she found nothing, no one. No clue who had been there. No horses in the livery, and the two wagons normally rented out were gone too.

The men caught up with her as she came out of the empty barn onto the street and walked toward the center of town.

"This place is a danged ghost town." Lucas scratched under his hat. "Where'd ever one go? It's almost like some witch or devil swooped down and hauled them all off."

"Stop that foolish talk. No such things. I can't believe a grown man even thinks such things." Rose gazed at Lucas. Fool.

"Well, my granny tells tales of such who are punishers from God."

"Could be, but hopefully these witches or devils only punish those who are evil and don't deserve to live."

"Will you two stop such stupid talk? We need to figure out our next step. We might try to find someone at home. All these folks might've just decided to lock up early and go home. So, let's go to some houses and check." Dell walked down the steps ahead of them, grumbling. "Witches, ghosts, angels, devils, goblins. The very like of such boggles the mind."

"I'm with you, but if no one is home at more than a few, then I'm riding out to fetch us some help. We can't do this alone. Maybe some of my friends — so-called outlaws — know what's going on here in Carlton."

"Let's go out to the farm where I found Guinn. The family who took her lived there. Maybe they just went back, thinking we wouldn't figure them to be there."

The approach of pounding hooves sounded loud in the silence. Dell hauled up short in front of her, and she bumped into him. Someone was riding down the street like his tail was on fire. She hugged the building along with Lucas and Dell and waited till the rider came where she could see who it was.

She leaped out of hiding. "Sam? Hey, Sam."

He skidded his horse to a stop and leaped to the ground. "Rose, am I glad to see you."

"Where've you been?" Her words tumbled over his.

"After the yahoos that did this." He pulled up his hat and showed her a purple pump-knot on his forehead. "Knocked me out cold for I don't know how long. Talked some before they did. I think they were headed toward Hawkins Post. I rode that way soon as I come to. They ain't seen no one this evening, but I give them the warning, then headed back here to see what they was up to."

Dell glared at Sam. "I see you're alive. Where the hell were you when they took Guinn?"

Sam appeared nervous around the sheriff who'd given him a badge. Probably guessed he would fire him. "I tried to stop them, but there was too many."

"No sense in worrying about that now. Tell us everything you remember," Dell said sharply.

"Two rowdies busted into the jailhouse just about when everyone was taking dinner. Most of the folk lock up and go home midday, leaving a sign on their door when they'll be back. The café stays open as does the livery 'cause they get business then. All I heard as they come in was one feller says, 'We going to mess with that Apache or not?' The other says, 'You ask me, I wouldn't want the whole tribe after me, but Dutch might have different ideas.' " He danced from one foot to the other before going on.

"Then they closed the door behind them and 'fore I can draw a gun one jumps right over the danged desk and wallops me one across the head." He pointed to the pump-knot. "I woke tied up, but I'm good with knots and purty limber, so I got loose in a while. Rode out to Hawkins Post to warn Julio. Saw nothing of them on the way, and he said he hadn't seen none either, so I come right back here to check what they might have done." He pounded his chest. "And here I am. I'm sorry, Sheriff. I didn't know about them taking your wife. I got no idea who they were or what they wanted."

Dell turned to Rose. "Who's this Dutch that feller mentioned?"

She shrugged. "Don't know one. Well, the only Dutch I know has gone to Mexico, I hear. Must be someone new in the panhandle."

Dell shook his head and looked like he wanted to hit someone. "Okay, so they went north but not to Hawkins Post 'cause of that Apache, Julio? Let's stop at some houses out that way and find out if anyone's seen them."

Rose scuffed her boots in the dirt. Looked up at Dell whose drawn expression showed his grief over losing Guinn again. She didn't usually disagree with him, but sometimes she had other ideas.

"If you don't mind, I'm going to ride out and find us some help while you do that. Been wanting to catch up with Wade for a while. He usually knows where to run down some real bad ones. Always has his ear to the ground."

"Wade *Guthrie?* I don't know, Rose. I see him again, I might have to arrest him."

"Surely not if he's helping find Guinn? You just said you'd lay down your badge to get her back."

He waved a hand. "Okay, you're right, go on. Find this Guthrie, and if he can truly help, well, fine. Hell, I'll give him amnesty or something. Where'll we meet you?"

She grinned. "Palo Duro Canyon, where else?"

"Now, Rosie, you're pulling my leg. That place is a beehive of outlaws. I don't want some ole boy taking a shot at us. Besides that's a fur piece. We need to do our searching near here. Find someone who saw what happened in Carlton. How about we meet at your momma's old place on the Red River? Then I won't have to come in guns blazing when I get there."

Wade's hideout being close, she agreed. But this hunt could well end up at Palo Duro where many outlaws hid. And it could mean going in guns blazing for that very reason.

Dell wasn't real happy to see Rose go her own way. She'd be real handy to have along. And what if she ran up against this gang? She wouldn't have a chance on her own.

Sighing, he turned to Sam and Lucas who were talking about what had happened. "Let's be off, boys. We don't want to be dragging folks out of bed, and it's getting dark."

Lucas unhitched his mare from the wagon. She was all he had to ride, so he went in the livery and borrowed a saddle from the tack room. Dell walked back up to the sheriff's office for Curly, and they were soon underway, headed out to stop at the first house. A few were scattered on the outskirts of town, and they'd go to them first.

Dell had his plans and was set on following them, hoping the other two men would agree. They seemed to want him to take the lead, which he was happy to do. He had to find Guinn before something worse happened to her. He could hardly bear to imagine what it might be.

A woman in an apron came out on the porch of a small farmhouse, the siding still smelling fresh from the sawmill. They were moving in quickly, these people who put up barbed wire around their property. Ranchers were up in arms, calling them sodbusters. They would continue to come, even to the panhandle of Texas, changing the way folks lived. Building houses on the prairie that was once free range for cattle. Since the war, it seemed everyone was headed west.

Dell had no reason to resent them but understood why ranchers did.

"What do you want?" the woman hollered, obviously unhappy about greeting three men she did not know.

He held up his badge. "Sheriff Hoffman, ma'am. We're looking for a woman who's been stolen from Carlton. Have you seen anything unusual, men passing by in a hurry today?"

"Oh, my. That's dreadful. No, I'm sorry. It's been quiet today."

"How about your husband? Was he out and about, perhaps mentioned anything odd?"

She turned, glanced toward the back field. "I — uh, no. I mean. Well, he hasn't come in yet. But he'll be here soon."

"Thank you. Ma'am, could I suggest that you stay inside with your door latched? Don't come out for any more strangers."

Gripping her cheeks with both hands, she stared wide-eyed. "My heavens, my heavens." She turned and hurried inside as if perhaps he could be the dangerous stranger he warned her about.

It was a longer ride to the next place, a small ranch running maybe a hundred head on a pasture between the two homes and off to the west. Bet he didn't appreciate the farmer so close.

A man on horseback met them halfway up a lane to the ranch house. By the time he drew close, the rifle he held cradled in the crook of one arm was obvious. Dell signaled the other two men to remain behind him.

"Good evening, sir. Sheriff Hoffman from Saddler County."

"Out of your territory, aren't you?"

"Looking for a woman, stolen from down in Carlton today sometime."

"Well, I haven't got her."

Hmm. A bit surly. Wonder what he has to hide? Best to be soft spoken. "This here is Sam Runkle, temporary sheriff of Carlton."

"Well, good luck to you, Sam. Last man there got himself shot."

"I'm a careful man. Have you seen anything odd today? A bunch riding by, hell bent for leather?"

Dell nodded at Sam. He'd stayed in control, too.

"Can't say as I have. Now I'll say good day to you and go in for supper."

"Thank you, sir." Dell touched the brim of his hat.

The rider reined his horse around and rode toward a house much larger than the farmer's and painted white. He'd never put the rifle in its scabbard as if he might need to use it momentarily.

"Sometimes you just can't find a friendly face." Sam turned from watching the rider to look at Dell. "Hope he isn't that unkind to his wife."

Dell glanced back over his shoulder. "Hold up. He didn't go in the house. He rode on around it and headed across the pasture. Let's get back over there. Wait till we've got the house between us and him before we go."

They followed his directions then tied their horses up on the far end of the porch out of sight of the disappearing rider. Dell led them to the front door and rapped softly. Something banged and crashed inside, and he shoved the door open, standing aside a moment. More banging then what sounded like a dog whining.

The three of them separated and covered

all the rooms. Dell found her in the kitchen, lying on the floor trussed up like a Christmas goose. So angry she was red in the face. He knelt beside her, worked the rag out of her mouth. She spewed and spit.

"Thank God, I thought no one would come. My husband, well, he. . . ."

"It's all right, ma'am." He introduced himself and the other two standing behind him.

She halted a moment like she might be considering something, then said, "My name is Norma Mason, my husband is Hugh."

"Who did this to you?"

With a sob she answered. "I don't know. I swear we have never done anything to anyone. I don't understand."

While he untied her, he addressed Sam. "Would you ride out and see if you can tell where that feller went to?"

Without speaking, Sam took off on the run. The sound of his horse galloping off set Dell to talking again. "How many of them were there?" He helped her off the floor and into a kitchen chair.

"They pushed their way in without waiting for me to go to the door. I thought they were going to kill me the way they talked and shoved me around. Only three of them, but there were more outside on horses. Who are they? What are they doing here?"

"We don't know yet. Was there a woman with them, did you see? Did they say what they wanted?"

"Could've been. I didn't get a good look at those outside. Said they wanted some paper I never heard of. They looked around in here a while after tying me up and gagging me. Went through some of my husband's papers, then left."

"Did they have on masks or cover their faces?"

"No, just as brash as you please." She broke into tears. "I thought they were going to kill me, or . . . or worse. My husband went to Amarillo yesterday, and the hands were out mending fence and looking for stray cattle, so I was alone and scared to death." Crying got the best of her, and she covered her face.

"You need to have the hands stay close till your husband gets home. And you have no idea what this paper was they wanted? Maybe something your husband might know."

"Do you think they're coming back?"

"Probably not, but it won't hurt to be careful." He didn't tell her they'd stolen Guinn for fear of frightening her worse.

Sam rode up and came inside. "He made a circle and headed northwest. Reckon Rose was right and they're going to Palo Duro?"

"Could be, but there's lot of country to the northwest. Places to hide. But that many in one gang, looks like someone would notice them, hear them, see them. Hell, this is as confusing as trying to work a puzzle with a piece missing. I'd like to know what they did down in Carlton and where all the people went to."

Sam scratched his head. "Sheriff, you know where we forgot to look? Where folks often hide when they're scared?"

Dell stared at Sam for a long minute. "Well? Say something. My mind is mush worrying about Guinn."

"The church, man. The church. Come on, let's get back there. I'd bet my bottom dollar that's where they went . . . or were put."

"Well, let's get back there then. You know none of this makes any sense at all. What are these men looking for? And why gut a town? And my poor Guinn." Though he tried to hold it back, a sob erupted from his throat.

Sam looked down at the floor. "Maybe only one of us should ride back to the church."

"That makes sense, Sam. The other two

can continue to search and try to find their trail. A bunch like that riding cross country might leave a trail we could follow."

Lucas cleared his throat. "Only one trouble with that. What would two of us do if we did catch up with them? We couldn't stop them. If we left to get help, they could get plumb away. I say we follow the most likely idea that all those people hid out in the church. By now they might've come out and gone on home. But there's a chance they could tell us what happened and why. This Miss Guinn you spoke of might be with them."

His words gave Dell hope. He turned to the woman. "Ma'am, you put on the latch, and, when your men come home, tell them what happened, and we said someone should stay here with you tomorrow. We have to go."

"Oh, do you have to?" Her brown eyes grew wide with terror.

Sam stood. "I'll stay with her till her men come in. You go on back to Carlton. I'll join you when the hands return. It's getting on dark. They'll be here soon."

"Thank you, thank you." She laid her head on the table, sobbing quietly.

Dell nodded his thanks at Sam. Rose was right about him. He stepped up when necessary. He'd definitely make a good sheriff for Legend County.

Outside he was relieved to see a huge moon climbing above the horizon. It would be bright as daylight out here on the plains once it rose into the dark sky. Bright enough to continue their hunt all night if necessary.

He climbed on Curly, and he and Lucas rode like the wind back toward Carlton and the church. How could he have been so dumb as to not have thought of the church? Still, he could only hope and pray Sam was right and they'd find everyone there, safe and sound.

Eight

Light from the rising moon caught up with Rose about the time the Red River shimmered like a giant snake across the landscape. All this illumination might be good for hunting, but for staying out of the sights of unfriendly guns, it could prove irritating. Maybe she ought to walk Cimarron along the hidden path to Wade's hideout, in case he had gun-happy company visiting him. For all she knew, he wasn't even here. If only she could make up her mind about asking him to help the law or just riding on, but all she'd been through in the past few days left her confused about what was best. Maybe just feel out his mindset before making a decision.

She hadn't dismounted when someone made the decision for her. "Climb down off that horse, mister, and don't think of using that gun."

If she'd learned anything to be true, it was

if you dressed like a man you were apt to be took for one, so she didn't bother correcting on that point. "Is that you, Wade, or one of your ornery friends?"

"Rosie? Well, gal, climb down here and come with me. Good to see you."

The outlaw emerged from the shadows along the riverbank. Even up close, finding his cabin was near to impossible. A deep cutback, thick with a growth of trees, offered a fine hideout for his cabin. She often found a few others of his nature spending time with him. Seeing her, bounty hunter that she was, they mostly cleared out before she could remember if they had posters out or not. She was sworn to give them time to disappear, being so close to Wade since childhood.

He mostly ran alone, only able to trust himself and her. Why he chose her to confide in, considering her leanings toward chasing his ilk was puzzling, but she never asked. It was a strange relationship, but they'd grown up as pals before either one took up a trade. Though he had a poster, she ignored it. If asked why, she simply shrugged. And about why he trusted her, he had no answer. It was one of life's mysteries.

Together they led their horses through the cut into a small corral at the back of the cabin. He gave them some grain, then took her hand. “Good to see you. What you up to riding around in the moonlight?”

Besides holding his hand, of course. “Just wanted to see you, that’s all.”

He kissed her knuckles. “Uh huh, and cows give chocolate milk. Who you looking for?”

“What makes you think I’m looking for someone? Maybe I just wanted to see you.”

“Okay, I might buy that, but first, uh, who you looking for?” He grinned to make it okay he’d asked.

“This is a crazy one. You’ll find it hard to believe.” While he poured them each a cup of coffee, she told him the story of an emptied town and Guinn’s double kidnapping.

“I’ll bet old Dell is fit to be tied.”

“He offered to throw away his badge and, as he put it, kill the son of a bitch who had his wife.”

Wade looked serious. “Sounds like him. I don’t blame him one bit. But why did you come looking for me? It’s strange to me how a town could get cleared out like that.”

“We . . . well, I was hoping you’d have heard about a gang big enough to do such a thing, since you get around a lot here in the panhandle. Who might be heading it up, running with them? Or you might even have some notion what it is they could be after."

"Sounds to me like they're after Guinn. Twice they've took her, you say. How'd he get her back the first time, or did he?"

"He did. I'm afraid he did something I never thought Dell would do. And it's killing him."

Wade set down his cup and stared at her. "Oh, he did what exactly?"

"He shot a kid who had snatched her the first time and had her tied in an extremely painful way."

"Now that don't sound like him. Shooting a kid?"

"He was pretty torn up about it. He hadn't pulled down when the kid pointed a gun at him. He was gonna shoot him, clearly, so Dell shot him. Like that. Killed him. He's been sorry about it ever since. I didn't tell you about that. It happened first before the town incident. This family had four boys who were out making trouble. They'd snatched me on the trail earlier and beat me up, so he went out to arrest them. The one wouldn't give up. He was young. Dell was having a hard time. After all that, the father of the boy comes and takes Guinn right out of their house. It's been a real mess even before this Carlton thing."

"Well, I reckon it has. There's a lot going on before the town clearing. Does he figure it's connected? Do you?"

"We don't have a notion. I came to see what you might think."

"Well, we can try to figure it out. You can stay here as long as you need. Did they hurt you bad? What I can't imagine is anyone getting the drop on you or the best of you in a fight."

"Huh, well, there was four of the boys, and they snuck up on me, knocked me out. If it'd been a fair fight, I'd a stood a good chance of whipping them."

He laughed. "Sorry for that, I know this is serious, but I believe you when you say that. You're one tough customer."

She held up a finger. "Don't you dare say for a girl, or I'll whop you. Those boys knocked me on the head till I didn't know up from down, but I'm okay now, thanks for asking. Listen, Wade. I don't want to hide from this. I want to help Dell. We thought you might give us a hand in hunting down this bunch. Now, I know how you feel about the law, but if you could make an exception. Dell has never come after you. He just turns a blind eye."

"Rosie, do you know what you're asking? I'd not be able to show my face around some of my friends if I helped the law run down some owlhoots. And it could get worse than that. I might be ostra . . . you know."

She leaned toward him, took his hand. "Ostracized. Not asking you to help run them down, but maybe you could poke around, find out if there's any talk about these ruffians and what they might be after."

"Don't go trying to charm me into this. I think a lot of you, but I won't betray these boys who trust me."

She let go his hand. "You have some idea who they are, don't you?"

"Let me put it this way. You and your friend Dell need to steer clear of this bunch. No, I do not . . . do not know precisely who they are, but there's talk about some of the worst low-down pieces of dirt to come out of Indian Territory forming a gang, and they have no boundaries. I hate to say so, but if they have Guinn, she's probably dead . . . or wishes she was."

"Oh, Wade. Don't you have any idea where they might be? Are they Indians or what?"

"Well, let's say it's a mixed breed."

"I think we ought to call out the Rangers or U.S. Marshals — maybe both — and cut them down. I wouldn't tell anyone you helped us."

"Lord, girl, I can't believe you suggested that to me. Everone knows our connection, they'd figger real soon it was me. I want to help, I really do, but, well, this is awful dangerous for all involved."

"I know it is, but I've never seen you back off from danger. I wouldn't have asked if it weren't Guinn they have. You are one of the good guys when it comes to life or death of the innocent and what's right."

"No, Rosie, I'm not one of the good guys. I'm a worthless bum who steals what doesn't belong to me 'cause I'm too lazy or too dumb to do otherwise. You'll need to offer your wares in trade to someone else for this one."

She jumped to her feet, knocking over the tin cup of coffee. "I did not offer my wares in trade. I can't believe you said that. I thought we were friends. So okay, if you're good to just sit around while knowing a gang of low down hoodlums and cutthroats are running around giving upstanding outlawing a bad name, well, then you sit here and do nothing while they maim and kill."

He laughed. "Giving upstanding outlawing a bad name? Is that what you actually said?"

She dropped back into the chair. "Okay, all right, you big dumb oaf. If that's what you think of yourself, I don't believe it for a minute. How much money do you have?"

"What? I don't know. Here let me see." He dug in his pockets and came up with two handfuls of change. Shrugged. "That's it. None buried in a fruit jar or anything like that."

"When was the last time you went out and robbed somebody?"

"Must've been a month ago. I — uh — guess it's about time I went out again."

"Wasn't precisely what I was getting at. If you're so serious at being a dyed in the wool outlaw, then you'd be robbing banks and trains and the like. Making something for your troubles. Is this what you really want in your life?"

"So, if I was worth my weight in gold, I'd be chasing down them who outlaw. Is that right?"

She paced the small room. "Well, I guess. Shoot, you know what I mean."

"How much you got in your pocket, bounty hunter?"

"Well, it's been a lean few months, and besides, I keep mine in a safe place, not my pocket where any owl hoot could hit me on the head and rob me anytime."

"In other words, about the same as me. Let's call ourselves even, then. I tell you what. If you can guarantee no one but you and me will know where you got your information, I'll see if I can learn more about these yahoos. We honest outlaws" — he gave her a big smile here — "hate to see men like them ruining our reputation. We'll have to arrange a way to meet up if I learn anything. How about if I leave something, not a message but a — playing card, say — but where?"

"You know that big rock out behind where Momma lived? Between Carlton and Thomas City, just at the edge of the woods. There's a hole toward the bottom on the outer side. Stick it in there. I'll go by and check, by myself, ever few days. Then we can meet in the saloon over at Hawkins Post. How would that be?"

He studied her closely. "Okay, if you promise. Now, sugar, let's get to what I hoped you came up here for."

She smiled, went to him, and put her arms around his neck. "I'm sure glad you're alone tonight."

He grinned and hugged her tight. "I am, too."

Lucas didn't say much on the ride back to

Carlton. That was fine with Dell. He was so worried about Guinn and the entire town of Carlton, his brain wouldn't stop spinning. One thing at a time. No sense in planning future steps before he knew the results of those in the present. Grateful for the light of the moon, he kept up a fast pace. It wasn't far, and they arrived soon without any bad occurrences.

Finally, the shadow of the church and its steeple rose in the distance against the night sky. He held up a hand for Lucas to stop. "Just in case there's some of this gang guarding over them inside, let's approach real quiet like."

Lucas nodded in agreement, and the two dismounted. Leading their horses, they sneaked up to the porch steps, tied them to the railing, and crept up to the entrance. Dell put his ear to the door, heard nothing, and very carefully shoved it open. Inside, sitting on the floor behind the back pew, was a youngster about ten or so. Dell put a finger over his lips. The boy started to rise.

Shaking his head, he moved toward him. When he got close, the boy broke and ran further into the church. "No, no." His whisper failed to reach the young man who had fled. From inside came a faint rustle, a vague feminine voice. Dell tilted his head.

If some of the gang was in here, they were deaf and blind. So, he took a chance he was right, stood and stepped into the room, identifying himself with his badge held out in front of his chest. He sure hoped no one hated lawmen. It'd give them a good target.

Instead came a woman's voice. "Oh, thank God, thank you, God. I thought we were lost for sure." She broke from the group huddled behind pews, stumbled toward Dell, arms out so he almost darted out of her path, but he stood fast. She threw her arms around him. Others rose from behind pews.

All he could do was search for Guinn among those coming out of hiding. One after the other and still his wife did not appear. He nearly cried out in anguish. Where could she be if not here? Why had they taken her? Would he ever see her again? His heartbreak blinded him with tears.

Excited conversations broke out as about two dozen folks gathered around to thank him. It was pandemonium for a while, and he let it finally die down while he brought his own emotions under control. Clearing his throat and wiping his cheeks, he held up a hand to signal silence. Maybe one of them had seen Guinn.

"If you all could sit down for just a moment, I'd like to ask some questions. We'll get you all home quick as we can. If you have the answer, would you mind holding up your hand, so everyone isn't talking at once?"

It took a while to accomplish that, but at last they managed to quiet down and sit there gazing at him. He felt much like a teacher caught in front of expectant youngsters. "Now, my first question has to be did any of you see my wife, Guinn? She would have been a prisoner of those who did this to you. So, a woman tied and gagged." He glanced at each face in turn, looking for some sign of having seen her. They all looked puzzled, some shaking their heads no.

"Red hair." He twirled fingers around his head. "Tall and beautiful."

One woman stepped forward and looked up into his face. "Sheriff, I'm so sorry these animals have your wife."

"Did you see her with them?" He could hardly catch his breath for the hope that sprung in his heart.

She shook her head. "None of them seemed to have any prisoners." She took it upon herself to turn and address the crowd. "Please, did any of you see a woman with this bunch?"

No, no, and no echoed from one to the other as their expressions turned sad.

"Why do you think they might have your wife?" The question came from a man holding onto a woman's arm as if frightened she might disappear.

"She was taken by a man whose son I shot when he drew down on me. It was a terrible thing for all of us. Then he came to my home and in front of a friend took her away. Now I'm searching for them, and I will find them. So, please, if you know or hear anything about this murdering crew . . . well, let me know. Now I need to ask some more questions so you can all go home. I know you must be tired. If you recognized any of the people who did this, raise your hands, and I'll get to each of you."

A few hesitant hands.

He pointed at a burly young fellow in a beat-up hat. "Sheriff, I know this happens some, that Indians are blamed, and I don't want to say that, but there was some of them in that gang. Not all, mind you, just some."

Agreement came over and over through the crowd.

"Thank you. That was very helpful."

Next, he pointed to a young woman, blonde hair pulled away from her face, then falling like silk over her shoulders, who stood from a pew when he pointed to her.

"Sheriff, I think one of them looked a little like a boy I went to a dance with last month. But he had — my boyfriend that is — has whiter teeth and a better haircut."

Dell expelled a breath. "Thank you, but I'm looking for you to know these people in the gang."

She shook her head. "No — oh no, I didn't mean it was him. I just thought you wanted people who looked like them, so you'd know. . . . I'm sorry."

"No, that's okay. I really appreciate it. Anyone else?" In some strange way he knew why she was confused. No one else offered help, so he asked them a few more questions about the experience itself and anything they might have overheard gang members say or if they'd stolen anything. Only the owner of the saloon answered that and said the whole gang wanted beer, and he gave it to them. They refused to pay, and he was afraid to insist 'cause they were so violent.

Nothing was helpful, so Dell sent them home. "I'm sure they won't be back here, but you have a competent sheriff in Sam Runkle, and he'll remain here and on the lookout now that we're aware what's going on. Meanwhile, in the morning, I'm organizing a posse to begin a search for this gang. We'll ride out toward Palo Duro where some outlaw gangs are known to gather. Any of you who might want to go along or know some who will, be at Sam's office by seven in the morning."

No longer able to hide his sadness, he turned away from the crowd milling to get out the door and stumbled to a pew where he sat and covered his face in prayer. After everyone was gone, the church quiet, Dell walked down to the railroad station, tapped on the window till Fleece came out of the back room.

"Hep you?"

"I need to send a wire to Thomas City." Fleece and Tabor Jones were brothers who worked at the depots in Thomas City and Carlton.

"Hey, Sheriff, sorry about your wife. Sure, write it here." He shoved a pad and lead pencil through the small opening in his window.

He read it aloud to Dell before placing a finger on the single black key, *"Deputy Kingsley – Gather men for posse leaving tomorrow before noon. I'll be there. Signed D Hoffman."*

Dawn rose in a flourish of color, the sun blooming in the midst of purples, reds, and golds of the Texas sky. A small group of men gathered outside the sheriff's office in Carlton.

Dell, who'd slept in a jail cell, emerged rubbing at a growth of two-day's whiskers and looking sleepy eyed. He thanked everyone for coming, stood on the steps and spoke.

"We'll be gone maybe a while, so any of you who need to be home for any reason, do so. I'll not think the less of you. I'm going up to Thomas City to gather more men, then we'll meet at Hawkins Post and cut cross country to Palo Duro. From there no telling where we'll go. It could be a long time out, so prepare your saddle bags accordingly. When you're ready come by here and put your name on the paper pad I'm leaving out here on the bench. I'm off to Thomas City. Lucas here will be in charge since Sam needs to stay here and protect Carlton in case those ruffians decide to come back. I've deputized Lucas. He's a good man. Listen to him. See you."

Without waiting to talk or answer questions, he climbed on Curly and galloped off. In Thomas City by midday, Dell left Curly at the livery with plenty of grain and walked back to the sheriff's office where town marshal Whit Burns, his day man,

Dutch Rothbury, stand-in, Fred Hanks, and new deputy, Gil Franklin, hired since the bank brought good standing back to Thomas City, were lined up on two benches either side of the door.

They all rose to their feet as one when he came in sight. Nearly together, they voiced their desire to be a part of the posse.

Waving a palm, he said, "I appreciate that. Someone has to be in charge here while we're gone. Marshal Burns, of course, is in line for that, but I'd like Deputy Kingsley to remain as well. I'll deputize Fred and ask Dutch and Gil to go along with me. Burns, you and Kingsley need to remain alert for any action by this gang and pull extra men in to help out if need be. We've got some capable help here, so make sure they know about what's going on and that they need to stand up, if necessary, while we're gone.

"Since this gang has already been to Carlton, for whatever reason I've yet to discover, I'm taking men from there for our posse. You'll see that this town, our town, is protected should they show up here. I asked Tabor to notify the rest of the towns along the railroad to be on the lookout. Word must get passed so folks can be prepared.

"Now, you need to pack your saddlebags for a long stay. We're meeting the rest of the posse at Hawkins Post soonest, so get ready. I'm going to the livery to get another mount. I've about ridden Curly down, and these men aren't worth the ruination of a good horse. Back here in an hour. Be ready."

Several citizens were out to watch the four men ride off, calling out to them as they rode out of town headed to Hawkins Post where Dell hoped to acquire the one man they needed the most, Apache Marshal Julio's cousin, Angelo, the best tracker in Texas and Indian Territory. He'd come in handy if they had to cross the border into the territory after this gang. Plenty outlaws, more white than Indian, hid out over there, and it caused U.S. Deputy Marshals to spend a lot of time in there, sent from Ft. Smith by Judge Parker to bring them back so he could try and hang them.

He didn't much care. White or red, whoever was doing this was going to be hung in Saddler County if he had any say in it at all.

And he planned to have plenty.

Nine

Wade decided to join Rose after all. As he put it, "I'll go with you and hang back out of sight of Palo Duro. Don't want anyone to see me with you. Later they could put it together that I helped bounty hunter Rose Parsons run down some of them. Along the way, I may ride off by myself should we run across someone who knows me."

"Not sure what help you'll be in that case, but I'll welcome the company. I do expect Dell to show up there, looking at some possibilities for this gang running wild over the panhandle. He'll have to be careful as well, since he's known by more than a few."

"I have a notion about this gang but would rather see for myself before telling you or Dell. There's been talk. They're giving a bad name to honest outlawry with their viciousness. But it puzzles me a great deal why they would empty out a town. I'm anxious to hear what all happened in Carlton."

"For one, they stole Dell's wife. And he's out for their heads. He will eventually ride this way, so you got any good friends hiding out in the canyon who are wanted for bad stuff, they'll be open game for both me and him. You do understand that, don't you?"

Telling him that went against her grain, but he'd feel betrayed if she didn't. Wade stared out across the prairie, a thoughtful expression on his face. "Sometimes it's awful hard walking the line between the law and what's right. But, by golly, it's not so hard to see the difference between good and evil."

She agreed about how difficult choices could sometimes be. She had a soft spot for Wade and perhaps understood him more than some did. He felt lost since his father was killed in the war, and his mother died of consumption. The two coming so close together sent him spiraling into his current outlawry. His mother tried to give him some purpose besides robbing folks, and so had Rose. He wasn't very good at it anyway. And what he took he usually gave away. Still, that was no excuse.

Wade reined in at a crossroad, one heading for Palo Duro and the other going over toward the Indian Territory. "I'm thinking we need to swing over to Cactus Junction. I have a feeling we might learn something there about this gang. If it's the one I suspect, and I'm saying nothing yet, you understand, they crossed into those Indian lands to hide out."

His words interrupted her thoughts. Though she heard what he said, she asked him to repeat it, just in case, and when he did, she agreed. He must have better than an idea about who they might be dealing with, so it was a good idea to stick with him.

"Okay, but I wish Dell and his posse was riding with us. This is dangerous, going alone there."

"Why, Rose, I didn't think anything scared you."

"I'm not scared, just cautious. Let the U.S. Marshals take care of that seething bog of filth that hides out in the territory and endangers the innocent women and children who are not allowed to go anyplace else to live."

"I never took you for an Indian lover, seeing as how they —"

"Hush that up, Wade Guthrie. Those women living with their babes in there had nothing to do with the scalping, burning, and killing done by Indians. Even the

Apache have settled down. Look at Julio and his cousin, keeping the peace in Hawkins Post. Now it's outlaws, many of them white and mean as rattlesnakes who are doing the harm. So why waste our time hating folks out of the past?"

He chuckled. "Okay, okay. Sure don't take much to get you up, does it?"

"You ought to know the answer to that."

Hawkins Post was quiet on the hot summer afternoon. Wade headed for the only saloon, and Rose followed. When he dismounted and tied his horse to the hitching rail, he glanced up at her.

"Just wait a while before you come in and don't show you know me. I'll see what I can find out. They won't tell me nothing with you hovering over my shoulder."

"Okay." She dismounted, tied Cimarron, and headed down the boardwalk away from the saloon.

"Hey, where you going?" He caught her arm.

"To see the marshal. I wouldn't be caught dead in the same place you're in." She pulled her arm free and stalked off, grinning.

Leaving Cimarron at a hitch rail in front of the leather shop on the shady side of the street, she strolled along peering in windows of shops, what few there were. For some reason, Hawkins Post had never grown much like most of the railroad towns. Not like Carlton and Thomas City, so there wasn't much to see. A saddle in the leather shop window, two new bonnets in a millinery no wider across than her arm span, a small mercantile, and finally, an open shed where the blacksmith worked. His thick shoulders and bare back covered in sweat, he hammered at a piece of metal glowing red from the coals.

After a while, she stood on the side of the street while a farm wagon carrying a man, woman, and three shouting children rattled past. Then she hurried across to stroll, now in the hot afternoon sun, in the opposite direction. There were few people out today, but they were a mix of Indians and whites.

Though the town was actually in Texas, the Indian Territory was within walking distance. She met an Indian woman who led her small child off the boardwalk and stood there till Rose passed before returning to the raised walk under the overhang of a man's hat shop. She moved on, wondering at such a world that made some honest folks better than others who were equally honest.

The door to Julio's small office stood open

allowing in what air was available, and she stepped in, removing her Stetson. He sat behind a well-used desk going through posters. That seemed to be a major occupation of lawmen, checking the most recent delivery of wanted posters to see who'd done what recently. She automatically leaned over to glance at the latest release. It was almost better than reading a newspaper.

He leaned back, locking his fingers behind his head. "What brings you to our fine town? What dangerous outlaw's head did you bring me? You may have to wait for the next stage's mail to collect your bounty. I am out of funds."

Though he could have been joking, his tone was short. There was a love/hate relationship between men of the law and bounty hunters. She never understood why. She helped them do their job without taking anything from them.

She didn't respond to his tone. "That's not why I'm here. Have you heard about the gang that cleared Carlton out the other day?"

He tapped fingers on the stack of posters. "Sheriff Hoffman was here earlier today. In fact, you only missed him by a little bit."

"Did he say where he was going?"

"Yes. Northwest toward the canyons. He

had many men with him. He borrowed my cousin, Angelo, to track for them. I was happy to oblige. Angelo grows tired of having nothing to do."

"Were you able to share any clues about who might be running that gang and what they wanted with an entire town?"

He shook his head. "Why do you care? Are you in search of new heads for your collection?"

"And if I were, it would save you the trouble."

He frowned. "They were all in the church."

"All of them? Even his wife, Guinn?"

"Ah, no. Sadly she was not among those found. None of them were hurt. He is very angry, and I am afraid of what he will do when he catches these men. Most especially if they have harmed her."

"You're right. But I'm afraid he'll do something bad even if she's okay."

"You may be right. Do you have a solution?"

"Sorry, no." She rubbed her hands down the front of her britches and rose. "Well, I'll be off. I think I'll try to catch up with them." She smiled to make it a joke. "Maybe I can get me a head or two out of that gang."

He deepened the scowl. "I would hope you do not bring them here."

Putting on her Stetson, she promised not to.

By the time she returned to the saloon, Wade was standing outside, one foot propped behind him against the front of the building. With a wide smile, she turned, pushed her way through the swinging doors and into the smoky, noisy, gloom of the saloon. The heavy heat smelled of spittoons and beer and sweat. Sounded of men bragging, laughing, and shouting. She elbowed her way to the bar and ordered a beer.

The bartender brought it and set it down, glanced into her face and continued to grip the glass. "No women served here, even if they be in britches and boots."

Hand cupped over the pearl handle of the Colt, she shook her head. From somewhere down the bar someone laughed.

Others joined him.

"That'll be five cents." His voice squeaked. With the other hand, she fingered a nickel from her pants pocket and laid it down.

"Sorry, didn't see who you was."

She nodded, still not saying anything, while she drank her beer. She wiped her mouth on the sleeve of her shirt, turned, and walked out.

More laughter followed her leave taking.

Wade had mounted up by the time she pushed through the swinging doors. Without speaking to him, she placed her left boot in the stirrup and swung onto Cimarron's back.

She waited to speak to him till they were out of town. "Okay if I talk to you now?"

He sighed. "Yes, Rose. Talk to me. Did you learn anything from Julio?"

"Not much. Dell's already been here. They found the townspeople in the church but still don't know what was going on. Julio doesn't know who the gang might be. Dell had a posse with him and took Angelo to track for him. I want to catch up to them. They're going to Palo Duro."

"I was afraid of that. Let's ride. How long ago did they leave?"

"Not long. Apache don't tell time, but he said we just missed them."

Before she knew it, Wade was lost in the dust of his horse's hooves, galloping off the trail to take a shortcut to the northern road to the canyons.

No telling what would come of this trip. An outlaw and a bounty hunter riding into a den of thieves who might or might not decide to shoot them both.

▪ ▪ ▪ ▪

Heading up a posse always gave Dell a feeling that he was in the wrong business. If being a sheriff was considered business. A posse often ended hanging a man from a nearby tree, something he couldn't condone. Yet, he had shot men down because they drew on him, giving him no choice.

These things he thought of each time he mounted up and led a bunch of men in search of a killer or bandit. An outlaw by any other name is still an outlaw.

Gil and Lucas, riding beside him, reined in when he did.

"Reckon he's still on the trail?" Lucas squinted into the distance at the vague figure of Angelo, returning to meet the posse.

Gil stared in the same direction. "Looks like we're headed in a direct line for the canyons of Palo Duro. Once in there, no telling what might happen. Out here on the prairie, you can see forever, but not in there, where there's mile after mile of caves, bluffs, cliffs, and outcroppings. Rock formations big enough to shelter a blamed army. There's places to hide and bushwhack us. We'd never see 'em coming."

Dell grumbled a reply. "It'd be good if you had a bit more confidence in our ability to put these guys down."

Lucas found that funny and chuckled. "Boss, I believe we can catch 'em, and if they don't give up, we'll take 'em."

Dell nodded at him. "Well, now, that's better." He glanced at Gil. "Ain't it?"

"Yes, Boss."

Angelo rode up, halting the conversation. A serious young Chiricahua Apache, he lived quietly with his uncle in the panhandle, while the majority of his tribe languished as prisoners of war. He apparently felt no malice toward white men individually, like Dell or Fred, Dutch or Gil, who had come along to represent the law, yet he carried out the tracking for a posse that might well go out after one of his Apache friends who didn't follow his peaceful trail. It must've made him uneasy. Still, there he sat in a saddle on his horse, like any of the men in the posse. A smile on his normally stoic face.

Dell couldn't help but admire him. Had he walked in the man's shoes, he'd have held on to a bitterness hard to swallow. "Surely you haven't picked up their trail so quickly. How do you even find the trail of an unknown gang with their horses stirring up the dirt?"

Angelo patiently explained. "Near Carlton, they gathered up. Having a palaver." Angelo gestured behind them. "There I found prints of horse-shoes with special markings. I do not track the gang. I track those few unusual shoes." He shrugged. "There, you know my secret. Perhaps you could track them yourself next time." He smiled broadly and returned to his work.

Gil settled the stomping of his horse. "What will we do if we catch up to them? It'll be a gunfight, won't it?"

"I 'spect it will. We'll do our best to come out winners." Dell spun his horse, a spotted Appaloosa he'd chosen to keep from riding Curly too hard, circled a hand in the air and shouted, "Ride out."

His order stirred the ten riders into spurring their mounts and following him at a gallop. Up ahead, Angelo led them. An amazing feat among the hoof prints on the hard-ridden road.

The sun followed them across the sky when they turned directly west on the main trail that more or less followed the Red River for a ways before it rushed north, a border between Kansas and the panhandle. The grasses had dried in the heat and drought of summer, the flowers long gone except for some drooping sunflowers.

It was out of those withering stalks, yellow heads bent as if in prayer, that the staggering figure appeared. Arms reaching out, toes dragging in the dirt till he could scarcely move forward. One of the posse tailing the others saw him, or they might have ridden on by. His shouts called a halt to the forward movement. Clouds of dust from the horses' hooves rose into the wind and whipped around their legs.

By the time Dell reached him, two other riders were on their knees staring down at him. He had taken his last step and fallen on his face — a bloody mass of stripped clothing and torn skin. Gagging was coming from his throat, as if the air or sound could no longer flow in or out.

Dell dismounted and grabbed his canteen off the saddle. "Help me turn him over. Easy now." Then spoke to the man. "God in heaven, who did this to you? Here, drink."

Holding the man, he helped him get some water in his mouth. Most came back out, a bloody stream that made Dell sick. The man was dying, that was clear.

"Tell me your name and what happened if you can. Someone did this to you."

The man's eyes rolled around as if searching for the sound of Dell's voice. He opened his mouth a bit. Tried to speak.

"Okay, take it easy." He turned to the posse. "Let's find some shade, make him comfortable. Here, four of you carry him." He pointed to a line of trees alongside the river. "In there. We can get some water to help him clean up."

He walked ahead of the four carrying their gruesome burden and, when they reached the sandy banks, had them lay him gently. "Now, go fetch some water in that coffee pot." When they returned, he had a spare bandana from his saddlebags, wet it, and tried to clean blood off the cut face. He could barely touch the man that he didn't cry out.

Feeling helpless, Dell knelt beside the horribly disfigured man and stared toward the river. At last a few distinguishable words came from the bloody lips. "Wahrgan" was what it sounded like he was saying. Dell bent close so his ear was close to the moving lips. "Wahrgan, misser, kill kill ife ife. Ssssh nuth nuth."

Try as he might, he couldn't make any sense of the man's words, if they were words at all.

With the setting sun they decided to settle in for the night under the shade of Bur oak and desert willow. The poor man clung to life with Dell hoping he might utter something helpful. Even as good as Angelo was, he couldn't track in the dark anyway. A full moon would be welcome, but the half-moon that would come up by midnight was scarcely enough to track by.

Lucas continued to doctor the man, getting a few swallows of water down him. Dell admired Lucas's patience, kept going by between setting up camp and checking on his progress.

"You know, Sheriff. I think he's saying Morgan."

"How does that help us?"

"Well, isn't there a Bull Morgan on a wanted poster in, uh, Sam's office? I saw it. He's done some bad stuff, I mean real bad. Now we find this guy while we're chasing a gang might be real bad."

Lucas stuck his hands in his pockets, his chest out. "Don't you think there might be a connection?"

"Oh, yeah, I remember that fella. He escaped prison down in Arizona. That Morgan?" Dell pulled the saddle off his gelding, slung it to the ground near the fire Lucas was building from widow makers he found scattered around under the trees.

Lucas nodded.

"It's a stretch. You're seeing things not there."

"Boss, he said this guy killed his wife. He said that."

"Okay, say you're right. That doesn't get us Morgan or the gang. Coffee would taste good. Let's get some on the fire."

Soon the men pulled out whatever their wives or mothers had wrapped for them to eat and a pot of coffee steamed on the fire. Lucas had gone back to sit beside the poor soul.

Emma Lou had wrapped bread and jerky and a small ball of cheese Guinn had made from the cow's rich milk for Dell. He had little appetite, but he ate anyway, the food tasting like old paper. She was a sweet girl, that Emma Lou, and would one day make some man a good wife. She took good care of Guinn after that family injured her. How he wished he could find her alive and unhurt. But the more time that went by, the more he faced a terrible truth.

She could be dead.

He lay on his back, head in his saddle, gazing at the stars that blurred through his tears. Talk died down among the men, and the camp grew quiet. One after another they began to snore. Out a ways from the eleven men lying with their heads on their saddles, sat a lone figure. The Apache, Angelo, still and straight, stared out across the prairie.

Dell didn't fall asleep for a long time. For he feared his dreams would be haunted by Guinn's suffering and what might be happening to her. He also feared he would dream what he would do to those animals when they caught up with them. And he had to face it. He didn't even know if they had taken Guinn. As far as Emma Lou saw, it was the father and uncle of the boy he'd shot and killed.

Someone shook him, called his name. He sat up, rubbed his face. In the light from a flickering fire, Lucas knelt next to him.

"What is it?"

"I think he's dying."

Dammit, this man was getting on his nerves. He rose, followed Lucas to where they'd laid out the man. Of course, he was dying. He had arrived right next to it.

He bent over and held a palm over his nose and mouth. No sign of breath. He lifted an eyelid. No life there either. "He appears to be dead. I'm sorry, there was nothing we could do but what we did."

"Well, I need to bury him."

Dell nodded. "Of course. Do me a favor. Go through his pockets and see if he's carrying anything that might tell us who he is or where he's from. Wait till morning and one of the men can help you with that. Now would you please let this poor man rest in peace and get to bed? Tomorrow is going to be a tough day for all of us."

Dell returned to his saddle pillow and sat down, arms around bent knees.

Ten

The heat of the day pressed down upon Rose like someone had dropped a great steaming hot blanket over her head. That wasn't exactly new in this country. She'd traveled through here often. But she'd never get used to this kind of heat. Even the shade was blazing hot. The wind was like it came from out of the open gates of hell on the devil's breath. She'd quit sweating in favor of broiling.

Colorado, her home state, was more to her liking, but her and Mama had left there many years ago in favor of Arkansas. For what reason she wasn't sure, but then Mama sold her business in Ft. Smith and moved into her little cabin outside of Carlton. They never really got along, and Rose stayed on the road most of the time. But she mourned Mama's death last year when that crazy arsonist burned her in her cabin.

Wade came back from a short scouting

and interrupted her thoughts. “Damn me if it ain’t hotter than the hubs of hell.”

“My thoughts exactly. We have plenty of water?”

“Yep, but there’s a spring in about three hours. Called Small Spring. Water always flows though.”

They rode without talking for a while before he broke the silence. “You think we’ll have any luck breaking up this gang of yahoos? If we do catch ’em, just exactly what have they done to be drug in?”

“Dell thinks they’ve taken Guinn. And they did hold guns on a few of the folks of Carlton and run everybody out of town.”

“But if all they took was a few beers, and he don’t know for sure they stole his wife, our sheriff has a posse out running down an unidentified bunch who might not have done nothing but have a joke on a small town. Don’t think it’s a jailing offense worth spending days in this heat chasing who we don’t even know.”

For some reason, Wade was always critical of Dell. She wiped sweat from her face with a bandana and stuck it back in her pocket. “Well, I’d bet if you thought there was a chance those outlaws had someone you loved, you’d be out here after them, now wouldn’t you? You could just go on home, wherever that is."

"Aw, Rosie. Don't get all het up on me. I was just speaking my mind."

"Well, don't. I want to stop in Thomas City and see if they've heard anything there about Guinn or this outlaw gang. I know Dell well enough to know he left some deputies in charge of his town. He could've wired back any news he might have."

"Julio said they were cutting across from there toward the canyons which means he won't be going through Thomas City."

"All the more reason for us to go that way. If there's been any news or something on the wire about this gang, we can carry the information on to Dell."

"Now that sounds like a good idea. Maybe we can have a cold beer before we light out for the canyons."

"I would expect we can."

In the late afternoon, they rode into Thomas City to find it in chaos. Men running here and there, shouting at each other, many carrying rifles, women hiding inside stores with their children, peeking out windows and doors.

In the street, broken bottles, on the boardwalks, shattered glass. Bullet holes in the sides of buildings, windows destroyed. A couple of shot dead horses lay near hitching rails. Up against the mercantile was what appeared to be a dead body covered in a tarp.

Spotting deputy Brand Kingsley rushing along the boardwalk toward the railroad station, she rode beside him. "What's happened here, Brand?"

But deep down, she already knew.

"Cain't stop this minute, need to send a wire down to Cactus Junction. It's real important, real bad."

She reined Cimarron in, swung down, and followed the deputy to the station, boots crunching on shards of glass. Inside, he dictated a message to Fleece Jones, who sent it as it came from Brand's lips. He was known to have the fastest finger in Texas.

Brand dictated, "Marshal Eben Hunter. Gang headed your way. Expect bad trouble. Sending men I can spare."

He turned and bumped into her.

"Can we do anything, me and Wade?"

"We could've used you both a few hours ago when that bunch hit us."

"*They* did all this? Who was it?"

"I'm thinking the same ones that emptied out Carlton yesterday. Don't know what come over them because this is way worse than herding a dozen or two folks out of town for the afternoon, like we heard happened down there. They was way wild here, as you can see. They was like a bunch of wild banshees." He walked as he talked, and she hurried to keep up. "We could use all the help we can get cleaning up this mess if you can spare the time."

"I reckon we can help the rest of today. We're on our way to catch up with Dell and that posse that's trailing this very bunch. God forbid there are two of them."

"Ain't that something? He goes off one way they come in the other, not two hours after he left here to pick up that tracker. Reckon he'll be following them here by tomorrow? This is plumb scary. Are they riding in circles or what?"

Dell wouldn't know about this until too late to help Cactus Junction. He was headed out across the prairie toward Palo Duro. She had to go after him, let him know.

Brand paused to gather some clothing out of the street. "Must be outta the ladies wear shop yonder." He gestured toward a neat little shop with broken windows and store stock flapping halfway out in the wind.

"I've gotta get back up to the office. I sent my only other deputy off with some armed men to try to get down there in time to help those folks defend themselves. This is the wildest thing to happen around here in ages." He turned to her, eyes blazing. "And, oh yes, I forget to tell you, they robbed our brand new bank before they left out. And they threatened store owners, told 'em if they wanted this to stop, they'd pay them every month to protect them."

Long legs eating up ground, she hurried to keep up. What was Dell going to think when he got this news? No way to tell him now that he'd headed cross country toward the canyon leaving the railroad and its wire facility behind. Not unless a rider could reach him.

She grabbed Brand's arm. "I can take him the message. Turn him and the posse back to help out at Cactus Junction. We've got to stop this."

Brand slowed down. Hands on hips, he studied her. "Rose, I know you're good on a horse, but —"

"Of course, I can do it, but it's the horse that counts, and Cimarron would rather run flat out than any other way. We can catch them."

"In this heat you'll run that horse to death."

"I won't. He's up to it. The best horse in the panhandle. These guys are getting worse every time they attack. They're liable to kill more than one down there. They only have a town marshal and a couple of deputies. I'm going. They've got to be stopped."

"Reckon I can't talk you out of it but take care."

"Find Wade Guthrie — he's over at the Water Hole — and tell him where I went, would you?"

"Sure, soon as I get a chance."

His last words trailed behind her up the street to where Cimarron stood hipshot in the shade on the far side of the buildings.

Obviously sensing her need to be underway, the long-legged Andalusian danced even as she stuck her foot into the stirrup, turning so she had extra momentum to swing into the saddle. She held him back until they left town, meeting a wagon pulled by two mules someone had commandeered from the livery to gather trash. Once they cleared all the commotion of the destroyed town, she leaned forward along his neck.

"Let 'er go, Cimarron. Let 'er go."

Ears perked to listen to her voice. He broke into the kind of gallop that had made him a successful rodeo horse. Running flat out, stretching those long legs, he was a horse that would run itself to death. She wouldn't allow that, but for now he'd eat up the ground.

Dell would surely beat himself up over

leaving Thomas City for a target. But choosing between pursuing the gang he believed had his wife and guarding a town he felt well-guarded may have made sense to him, seeing as how he was nearly wild with fear for Guinn's safety. Rose didn't blame him for making the choice he had, but some would. So would he. Even if he saved Guinn, he would never get over it. She knew him that well.

The wind in her face cooled a bit now that the sun dropped toward the horizon, but it would be hot till dark slipped across the flat prairie. The valiant bay kept up the gallop till she slowed, then stopped him. Small Springs had a sign out telling the water was good. Even off the main trails such information was important. She allowed Cimarron the pleasure of walking out into the bowl of water on the downside of the spring where he wouldn't stir mud into the clear water flowing in. Let him drink a bit, but then she led him away. Once this run was over would be time enough for him to drink again.

For several minutes she stood with him in the shade where a breeze helped a bit. Rubbing the soft muzzle, she spoke. "It's time to let 'er go again, Cimarron."

He nodded his head and made a sound deep in his throat. When she placed her foot in the stirrup, he turned and was moving before she placed the other. He was still doing fine and would for a while. If only she could catch Dell before he gave out. She would not run her horse to death for all the people in ten towns. Regardless of what anyone thought.

Soon sweat foamed from around the saddle and across his withers. As far as she could see no riders were visible in the distance. Cimarron began to chuff, and she drew him up near some trees, climbed down, and let him walk in a circle around her till he cooled down. Wiping his withers, she carried on a conversation with him.

"How do you feel, fella? We don't catch 'em soon, I'm stopping. What do you say?" He looked deep into her with big brown eyes, and she rubbed his forehead, then his neck.

Dell wouldn't be rushing the posse, either. Riding flat out in hot weather could be disastrous, and anyone worth their salt knew it. A man left on foot would die. She kissed Cimarron's soft nose.

"What do you say? One more go?" He stomped around, hooves cutting clods. "Okay, okay."

It would be the last time. He no longer turned his anxious circle but waited for her to mount and touch his flanks with her heels. Then he was off one more time, but his pace told her he was tiring badly.

Maybe ten minutes later, she came over a slight rise, and there in the distance, so far off it appeared as a gathering of ants, rode what had to be the posse. If Dell and the good folks of Thomas City ever caught that gang, there'd be hell to pay. If they didn't, it would be worse than that. But Cimarron was done, and she would ask little more of him.

"Once more, baby." He turned and moved out. One more spurt, but after another few minutes or so, she hadn't shortened the gap between them. She drew up, pulled her rifle from its scabbard, took aim, and cut clods behind the horses, levering and pulling the trigger over and over.

Between her legs the big horse took heavy breaths. She rubbed his sweat soaked neck. "It's okay. We did it. You did fine." She would not ask another step out of him this day.

The shots echoed, filling the air with booms, and at last, Dell called a halt. There was a danger they'd shoot back, but she had no choice. Once they stopped, she stood in her stirrups and waved her Stetson as high as she could reach, then waited for them.

He was sure to recognize the big Andalusian and know it was her. Or one of the men would shoot her.

The shots slapped the air around Dell. Even underway, with the thudding of dozens of hooves, heavy breathing of the horses, his own sucking air into his lungs, the gunfire brought them all up short, some scattering to avoid being hit. All that and the multiple booms overcame all other noise.

Dell dismounted his still moving horse, rifle in one hand, eye out for a place to take cover. It was as if someone rained rocks in their direction. Once on his feet, crouched in a low spot, he scanned the terrain. A large bay horse on the rise behind them, someone standing in stirrups waving a Stetson. Once he had the fight or flight reaction under control, he could concentrate on what he was seeing.

Rose and her magnificent horse. He leaped to his feet, shouting, waved his rifle above his head, yelled, "Hold your fire! Hold your fire!" Some of the posse fired off a shot or two before he could stop them. There that crazy woman stood, crossways of the trail, having sent her horse trotting away. Just like her to worry about him getting shot but not herself.

No telling what had happened, but it was something important, or she wouldn't be out there.

"What in thunder's going on?" This came from among his men, he couldn't recognize who. Probably stated what most of them wondered.

"It's Rose Parsons. Probably needs to tell us something important."

"Oh, yeah, sure. The bounty hunter probably wants to hold us up till she can get ahead of us and catch some of these ruffians."

He walked through the milling men, leading his mount. "I'll go see what she wants. You can all take a rest. Give me a minute."

He wasn't happy about the grumbling that followed. It never took much to turn a bunch of men from good to bad if they suspected chicanery. Two or three with stupid remarks would do it. He had to find out quick what was going on.

She came to meet him, leaving the bay munching on dry prairie grasses, reins hanging to the ground. "Sorry about that, Dell. I had to stop you. Cimarron was wore out, and I couldn't push him anymore. The gang that hit Carlton hit Thomas City this morning. Now they're on their way to Cactus Junction." She held a hand over her chest while she took several breaths.

"That's not good, but it's not enough for you to put your life at stake like this. One of us could've shot you."

She held up a hand. "Hush, Dell. Let me get a breath." He did, and she did. "It's really bad. They killed someone, shot up all the buildings in town, robbed the bank, and now they're headed to do the same or worse in Cactus Junction. You needed to know to turn around and come back. Maybe you can get there in time to help them. Or, if not them, the next town they put in their horrid plan. Or maybe just run them down and shoot them. That may be the only way to stop them."

"What the hell is up with them? Does anyone have any notion who they are? Anyone in Thomas City?"

"I don't know. It's some sort of paid protection. When I heard where they were headed, I knew I needed to stop you going to the canyon and get you headed down to the junction. They'll be there by morning."

"We can't be there by then."

"You can if you get fresh horses. You can ride all night."

"Where the heck we getting fresh horses?"

"The Buckle D is about five miles that away." She pointed. "And we helped save his ranch and family from the arsonist. Remember? He's got fine horses. We can leave these and use his. I know he'll let us."

She was right, and it was a great idea. With a frown, he nodded, sorry he hadn't thought of that solution. But she'd had time to mull over their problem and seek an answer.

"It can't be far to his ranch." Dell double-timed it back to his men, some of whom had dismounted and were gathered, discussing the delay in loud voices. "Okay, those owlhoots are on their way to Cactus Junction, and we've got to get down there to help those folks. We're stopping at the Buckle D to see about exchanging mounts temporarily, then we're riding all night. Any of you don't like it, ride out now, but stop making trouble. Now mount up and let's get moving." He rode out ahead setting the pace.

Everyone stuck. Maybe they had friends and family down at the junction, or maybe they just didn't want to look like cowards by running away. He didn't care, long as they stayed with the posse and didn't make any trouble. Rose brought up the rear, falling a bit behind as she pampered that horse of hers. You'd 'a thought he was her family or something.

Lamplight glowed in the windows of the

Buckle D ranch house, a welcome sight to the weary posse. Ordinarily coming upon a place like this after dark would mean stopping for a few hours' sleep in their barn, but not this time. Somewhere out there that gang of ruffians was on its way to destroy, maybe even kill. And folks needed help.

A dog barked to greet their approach, and someone came out on the porch. "Who is that? I've got a gun."

Dell always got a charge out of that. Wanted to say who didn't? But he refrained. "Mister Dawson, it's me, Sheriff Hoffman from over Thomas City way. We need to talk, and we don't have much time."

"Then get down, and let's do that."

"I've got a posse here, eleven of us to be exact. We're on our way over to Cactus Junction. We've learned a gang, the same one that hit Carlton yesterday, is on their way there after tearing up Thomas City this morning and robbing the bank."

"Sorry to hear that, but what's it to me?"

"Well, sir, we've run our animals too fast, too long. We'd like to exchange our mounts for some of your fresh horses, temporarily, of course. Once this is settled, we'd be right back here with them."

"What sort of a guarantee do I have of that?" Buck Dawson sounded downright unfriendly.

"Well, sir, I *am* the law. Do you think I'd condone stolen horses?"

"Maybe not, but suppose some get shot or drop dead from running in the heat. What then?"

Should he remind the man of last year when Dell carried his wife out of the fire? Or how his neighbors had shown up to help him rebuild the house after? Hated to have to do that.

Rose rode up on her bay. "Maybe he doesn't remember what you did."

"Looks like it. Either that, or he just don't care. I'm just glad you got here, gal. Thanks for doing what you did. I'm afraid I'd be halfway to the canyons by now if you hadn't."

The front door squeaked open, and someone came out on the porch. A woman's voice spoke for a few minutes with the man interjecting a word here and there. A short length of silence, then he spoke. "Horses are put up for the night in the barn. I'll go with you, and you can pick the ones you want. I'm sorry I was hesitant." He chuckled. "Wife keeps me in line when I'm thoughtless. Let's get out there and fix you up so you can be on your way. Might I join your posse? Some of those folks over there were kind enough to help us out after the fire, as she was quick to remind me. Leave it to a woman to straighten things out."

Dell stifled a chuckle. "Of course, we welcome you. It's going to take a lot of us. There may well be gunfire."

"Then, I'll bring along a gun. Go on to the barn, choose a mount. I will join you soon."

A flash in the sky spooked some of the horses on the way to the barn. Here and there, men settled them down, but the boom that came and literally shook the ground sent them all scrambling again. Dell, being on a green broke gelding he wasn't accustomed to, was busy calming the nervous animal. It took a while to coax them all into the barn, drag off their saddles and bridles, and choose another from the stalls.

The storm hit with a vengeance, rain pounding the roof before they could ride out. Most of them had brought along rain gear, and so they took the time to don the waterproof dusters. This was taking forever. Would've been better if they'd ridden on by, taken a chance on getting there on the horses they rode. Maybe even have beaten the storm.

Finally, the doors were opened, but by then, seeing was impossible. Dell cursed under his breath.

"No use in going on in this," more than one of them grumbled.

Buck dismounted. "Ain't room in the house to put you all up, but the haymow up above would be comfortable and dryer than it is out there. Nobody's going nowhere or doing any raiding in a storm like this."

Guinn was going further and further out of reach. Anger like a fire rose to blind Dell. No storm was going to stop him going after her.

"What in thunder's going on?" someone shouted.

"Sorry, sorry." He stopped kicking the stall siding and slid down the corner post to the floor, holding a hand over his eyes. If he didn't get her back, he didn't know what he'd do. She was the best woman in the world. He loved her more than life itself. But here he was, thinking of himself. No telling what she was going through, hoping every minute that he'd rescue her. If she was alive. Dear Lord, what if they'd killed her already and him riding off in the wrong direction?

While the chattering posse climbed the ladder into the loft, he remained sitting on the dirt floor listening to the thunder and rain. It was one of those Texas frog stranglers that showed no hint of stopping. At least he could hope it would keep that gang from hitting Cactus Junction. But what if they turned to another entertainment? His Guinn, for instance. If they so much as touched her that way, when he caught up with them, he was taking off his badge.

Someone stood over him, and he took away his hand to stare up at Rose, hands on hips. "You want to go? I'll go with you. We've never let any old storm stop us pursuing law breakers. Neither one of us. And she's out there."

He scrambled to his feet, went to the horse he rode in on, still saddled and standing. "No need you going, Rosie, but I can't stay here. It's driving me crazy thinking of her in their hands."

He dragged out his rain gear, wrestled into it. She was doing the same, still holding the reins of the horse she'd followed them on. "Me either. Let's go."

Buck swung the door open to let them out. "You're both crazy."

Rain hit so heavy it almost choked him, yet he urged the horse out into it. Head down, he turned toward Cactus Junction, Rosie right behind him.

"We're coming, Guinn. We're coming."

Together they'd make it or die trying.

Eleven

Hat pulled low over her face to block the rain, Rose followed Dell by letting her horse do the job. The borrowed Appaloosa kept his nose almost touching the hind quarters of Dell's mount. Both plodded on, as if saying okay, humans, we'll give it a try.

How in the world was he keeping from going in a huge circle? Left up to her, they'd end up back at the barn or wandering all over the prairie. Rain poured off the front brim of her hat like a waterfall. That it covered her eyes wasn't a problem since she had no idea where they were going.

Okay, something had happened, for suddenly there wasn't much rain around them. He'd led them into some sort of shelter. She shoved back the Stetson to see where they were. Trees surrounded them, keeping out the worst of the rain.

He turned to face her and raised his voice.

"Let's stop here for a bit and get our bearings."

She was more than happy to do so. "I can't see a thing in any direction but rain, lightning, and — oh, wait, look that way." She pointed. "Wait for the lightning. Keep looking."

Sure enough, the shadow of a building. "Let's go there and ask where we're at. There must be someone at home. Who'd be out in this weather, anyway?" She laughed at her joke, trying to keep things light for him. It must be hell not being able to help Guinn. He adored her. She couldn't imagine how it must feel.

"Not funny. There's no lights, but maybe they'll forgive us waking them, seeing as how we're lost."

Just as the words came from his mouth, a shot sounded, the bullet zipping past her ear.

"Guess they do mind. Better get on away from here before they improve their shooting abilities." He kicked his horse's flank and rode out of there.

Rose followed quickly but hollered at the marksman. "You hadn't ought to shoot till you can see we're not here to harm you."

"*Git!* Git off my place 'fore I don't miss."

"Tell us where we're at." Dell had ridden

around the end of the building where he tried again.

"Dad blamed, you trying to get yourself shot or what?"

"I'm Sheriff Hoffman from Saddler County. We're looking for the road to Cactus Junction."

"What the hell's the matter with your brain? Cain't you see how bad it's storming out here?"

By this time Rose had reined up behind Dell and out of range of the shooter in the front window. "What's the matter with that fella, anyway?"

"Probably some old hermit just wants to be left alone. If I could just get his name, I might be able to figure where we're at."

She slid down off her horse. "Let me try the feminine approach."

"Rather you didn't, Rosie, let's just ride on."

"Aw, let me try, I'll be careful." Hugging the outside wall, she slipped around next to the opening where the shots came from. A whirling gust of wind slammed the rain over her, pinning her against the house. "Mister, really, we're lost and looking for the town of Cactus Junction. Which way is it, and we'll get out of your way?"

He stuck the rifle barrel out the window.

"There, go that way. And forget you ever saw me here."

Carefully she sneaked back to where Dell waited, turned, and pointed. "It's over that way." She climbed on her horse and headed in that direction. Maybe they could find an honest rancher out in that mess who would actually send them in the right direction. Sure seemed that fellow wanted rid of them awful quick.

There was no sign the storm or rain was slacking off. Wind whistled and battered them. Lightning and thunder played tag with ugly dark clouds. Sheets of water, hard to see through. A wonder they didn't get blown plumb off their saddles and drowned in the puddles. Still Dell kept moving, and she had no choice but to follow. He was all she could see, so she might as well go with him. It sure beat ending up out here alone. But not by much.

A slight mound off to their left forced the horses to turn right, and before Rose could rein her frightened mount in, she was stirrup-deep in rushing water. Dell was nowhere to be seen in the pouring rain, and she and the animal between her legs went under. Sliding from the saddle and off his back, she grabbed his tail. There was no choice but to let him swim and hope they would come out on solid ground. Rushing water washed over her face, choking her. Both hands began to slip loose from the wet hair. The strong horse had a better chance of surviving in this wild surge of water. She didn't, so she tightened her grip, one hand at a time. She couldn't get any wetter.

No idea where Dell might be, nor could she spot him in the melee that surrounded her. Dear God, she could only hope and pray he would survive, even if they couldn't find each other. This storm wouldn't last forever, but the flash flood would keep flowing and her and the horse with it till perhaps it would wash them up onto solid ground. With no idea where she might be, she let the water take her wherever it chose.

She went under, flailed to the surface, and lost the horse. Just like that, the animal surged out of sight, and she was all alone. The lonely, endless prairie was hiding somewhere out there in the dark. How long this had gone on she couldn't imagine. But soon the flash flood would race downhill and dump her into the Red River. Somehow, she had to get out before that happened. All she could do was pick a direction and make her way to the shore. She finally chose the right and began to swim as strongly as she could toward whatever awaited her. For every foot she made, the water carried her even more feet straight ahead.

She thunked into something hard, something floating. It lurched up and down, scraped her cheek raw. When she spread her fingers along its surface, there was tree bark. Exhausted beyond taking another stroke in the angry water, she threw both arms over the huge trunk and rested her head there above the choppy waves. After a while, she managed to fight her way forward till the floating tree was under both arms. Past any more effort, she rode the bobbing tree wherever it might take her. Her energy was exhausted, and it was up to the tree to find a way for both of them.

During the time of her efforts to keep from drowning, the storm and rain lessened, then stopped. Hanging in the clearing sky was a sickle moon, a bright star close to its lower tip. For a moment she was gripped by the sheer beauty of the sky, while one by one, stars appeared to sparkle brightly. She could almost forget where she was if she hadn't been so soaked, tired, and hungry.

Without warning the racing log hit something, swung, and threw her into the air. She came down with a solid thump on muddy ground. She lay there dazed, seeing stars of another kind. No telling how long she remained on her face in clods of prairie grass before coming around. After four or five tries, she managed to stay on hands and knees. It took another few to climb to her feet and stagger around before getting her bearings.

What a strange and frightening experience. Almost made her think for a moment it had all been a dream and she would awaken in her own bed. That is, if she wasn't so wet and still wearing rain gear. She shrugged out of the oilcloth coat, dropped it on the ground, sat on it, and took off her boots. Dumped water out of them. Took off her socks and wrung them out. Soon she shed all of her outer clothing and spread each piece on some bushes. The air was tepid. Everything would dry when the sun came out. Meanwhile she would try to learn where she was. She'd just lie under the bushes a few minutes.

She opened her eyes to brilliant sunlight. Where was she? How did she get here? Rising to see the trickling stream, it all came back. The adventure, then her crawling out of the flash flood that now was no more than a new-formed wash. She must've fallen asleep wearing only her underthings. On nearby brush, her clothing flapped in a breeze. One by one she gathered her britches, shirt, and bindings and dressed. Counting the bruises all over her body from the wild water ride she'd taken. How had she survived?

At last ready to head out, she gazed upstream for a long while in the hopes she'd see Dell or his horse or hers. No sign of anyone or anything but washed clean prairie. Relieved to feel the sun, she headed back in the way from which the stream had washed her. At least she had something to follow, but how would she tell when she reached the point where the two of them had been sucked into the flood? He surely survived, strong as he was. Maybe she'd have to figure out where she was when she got there. If she ever did.

The thing he hated most was losing Rosie to the vicious water. It had happened so fast. One minute she was there, the next gone. She hadn't screamed or made a sound that he could hear over the storm's noise. The flash flood roared toward them, something he'd experienced before. He yelled at her to follow him, and he rode to higher ground, the horse's hooves digging into the muddy escarpment till they reached a tree covered rise. There he rode out the storm, calling for her desperately all through the night.

With the rising of the sun, he rode the debris loaded bank down to where the waters had dumped into a good-sized stream and swole it out of its banks. With tears in his eyes, he kept up the search for a while, but the fate of another woman called to him, and so he finally sadly gave up and rode toward Cactus Junction. He could only hope that the gang had run into as much trouble with the storm as he and dear Rosie. He had to make it there before those yahoos tore another town apart. It was time to stop them.

All the way to Cactus Junction he rode with an eye out for lost Rosie as well as trying to catch members of this gang wreaking havoc on the good people of the panhandle. Back on the main trail, there was some traffic. He stopped a man riding out from town.

"Naw, nothing happening there when I left this morning. Seemed more people than usual, though."

That perked his ears up. "By people, you mean riders or families coming in wagons to buy necessities?"

"A little of both."

"Is the town marshal there? Someone needs to ride out and fetch Sheriff Sam

Runkle. Cactus Junction is his jurisdiction."

The man shook his head. "There was a deputy there, don't know his name. I live up at Hawkins Post so don't know some of these fellers. You 'spectin' trouble?"

"Hope not. Got to get on my way."

He left the man in the middle of the trail, watching him with a puzzled look on his face. He sure didn't have time to explain or ask any more questions. Sounded like the gang might be there but just hadn't started anything yet. He kicked his horse into a gallop. The town would soon be filled with the posse he'd left in the haymow of that barn. They'd probably catch up with him before he got there.

And they did. Hoof beats pounded the ground, approached before he reached the outskirts of Cactus Junction.

He waited to talk to Deputy Dutch Rothbury, a natural born leader, who had taken the reins, so to speak, with that posse when Dell left them in the barn. He had them pretty well whipped into shape since the previous night.

"You didn't happen to see Miss Rose anywhere, did you?"

"No. Where'd she get to? That was a mighty fierce storm y'all left in." Dutch sounded concerned.

"I'm afraid she might be drowned. Don't know for sure."

"Lord a'mercy, Boss. How'd that happen?"

"I haven't got time to tell you right now. Let's get on into town so we can set up a good defense against those outlaws headed this way."

A good while later, Dell caught sight of the town and halted the posse.

"Now, I'd rather they didn't know about us when they ride in. If they're already there, they'll likely act the same as in Carlton and Hawkins Post. Set around drinking beer in a saloon till they swaller down enough courage. So, Dutch, I want you to take three men and post 'em at the back of the buildings on the north side to cover. Gil, you take three and close off escape out of town on the main road. I'm going to pick three for the south side of town and leave a man here to let us know if they turn tail and try to run. I'm going to do some stirring in town. I want 'em took down for good and all fore they do anymore damage. They come out firing, it's shoot to kill. Look out for a woman. If my Guinn is a hostage, don't shoot.

"Now, let's get moving, men, 'fore we run out of time. Stay out of sight and make every bullet count. Let them start it."

Once the men were all in place, Dell rode into town casually. He may have looked like he didn't have a care in the world, but he sure did. His sweeping glances took in every man, woman, and child on the street. He sure wished he had more men. What had happened to the posse from Carlton was a puzzle. Perhaps the storm played havoc on them.

Time crawled, and nothing happened. The town remained peaceful. Somehow, they must've heard what was going on here. That gave him the time he needed to warn folks. He went into the bank first, introduced himself, and asked to see the president.

A youngish man with a receding hairline and a gold pocket watch in his fancy vest greeted him. Held out a hand. "I'm Percival Cramer, sir. How can I help you?"

"You're probably going to be robbed today, Mister Cramer. Do you have any security hired?"

The man's eyes widened. He pointed to a large young man standing behind a potted plant by the door. "He's our guard. But if you're a sheriff don't you have men? Deputies?"

"I have some, and we'll assist you as much as we can. But I suspect that my wife is being held by members of this gang, and so I'll be concerned about rescuing her as well. You must understand my concern may outweigh my worry about a bank robbery."

"Oh, dear me, I do. You tell us what to do, and we'll do it."

"I appreciate that. I would imagine your establishment will be their main focus. I'm expecting more men to arrive to help out. We'll do what we can to prevent folks from getting hurt. Just do what they say, give them the money, and we'll do our best to get it back before they leave town."

"I will instruct my staff to cooperate with them, Sheriff. Lives are worth much more than all the money in my bank."

Dell worked his way down the boardwalk instructing each business manager and their clerks how to react to the gang. "Go and hide because you can't stop them. There's going to be lots of gunplay, and I don't want anyone hurt." These were the instructions he gave them one and all. It was important he not have these people firing on a gang that could very well have his wife in their midst.

It was after midday when folks meandered back into the street from eating something that the gang burst out of three saloons nearly at once. They started down the street shoulder to shoulder, shooting and shouting. Window glass shattered, women screamed, men hollered. What a mess.

Dell motioned to his men to move in and take care of business. There must've been upwards of a dozen of them, carrying pistols and rifles and shooting without a care who or what they hit. "Okay, we need to pick a target, take it down. None of this just shooting wildly and hoping to hit something." This he had made a point of with them, but had they listened?

Yes, the gang was beginning to fall as they advanced down the street toward the bank. Clearly the gang of outlaws hadn't expected what was happening. Gunmen picking them off from hiding.

And no one expected what happened next. It was like the arrival of the cavalry. The posse from Carlton rode in. The gang never made it to the bank. After two or three more of them were brought down, the rest threw down their guns and surrendered.

Still, where was Guinn?

Dell waded through the fallen to get to some five men who had given up when the second posse arrived. One of them was the man whose son he had shot what seemed like an eternity ago. He went at him with a madness he didn't know he possessed.

Grabbing his shirt front and shouting into his face.

"Where's my wife, you son of a bitch?"

The man exposed his yellow teeth in a gruesome smile. "Don't you wish you knew? Maybe she ain't with us no more. Maybe we throwed her in a ditch or in that flash flood that come through in the night. Wasn't that something?"

Dell shuddered down to his toes, a hatred for what this man stood for rose up in him like bile. And he hit him across the face, one way then the other, with the barrel of his six-shooter. Blood spurted from the man's nose, and a gashing of blood opened across both cheeks.

Dell stepped forward, more than ready to do worse, when, in the silence following the gunplay, someone shouted his name.

He halted, looked around. "Dear God, that's Guinn. Where did it come from? Guinn!"

He turned as the shout came again. Out of the bank came Percival Cramer with one arm around a stumbling woman. A man supported her from the other side.

"Sheriff, sir. I believe we've found your wife. They left her in the bank tied and gagged in the back room. She says they were going to use her to rob the bank once they finished destroying the town."

Guinn spotted Dell about the same time he spotted her. She started toward him, the two men hurrying along to support her while Dell fought through the crowd in the street, part outlaws, part posse, and part townspeople. He wanted to go back and do more damage to the man who had arranged all this, but he wanted worse to put his arms around his wife and hold her close. They met in the street, and that's exactly what he did.

She cried on his shoulder, trembled in his arms, tried to tell him what happened but couldn't get out the words.

"Shhh, shhh, Guinn. It'll do to tell later. I want to take you home. Put you to bed, make you soup, dry your tears." He swept her up into his arms and carried her down the street. At the livery, he rented a horse and wagon, made her comfortable in the bed with blankets supplied by Ray Conte, the liveryman, then climbed up in the seat and drove to where all the people milled around, not sure what to do next.

He reined the horse in and stood on the seat where everyone could see and hear him. "I've found my dear Guinn, and I need to take her home. So, Sheriff Runkle, where are you?"

Sam stepped forward out of the crowd and tipped his hat. "Sure proud you found her, Sheriff."

"I need you to handle getting this sorted out, would you? Dutch is a good hand to rely on. He's one of my deputies in Thomas City. Put these yahoos in the local jail and wire Judge Needham. He'll instruct you what to do. And get a couple of your boys to try to find Miss Rose. She was caught up by the flash flood northwest of town about five miles." He paused, stared down hard on Sam. "Sorry to say, you may be bringing home a body, but can you do that for me?"

Before Runkle could ask, Dutch and Gil stepped forward, and both said they would go on the search.

Dell shook his head. "Dutch, you need to stay here and help Sam handle things. He's new to the job. Gil, you shanghai one of the posse members to help you look for Miss Rose." For a couple of minutes, he explained to Gil about where they were when Rosie went in the water. A knot rose in his throat, and he swallowed it down. He admired Rosie and had grown fond of her, too.

"We'll find her, Sheriff. We sure will." Gil leaned near Dutch and said something Dell didn't hear. When Dutch shrugged, he turned to Dell. "Sheriff, where shall we —

uh — take her body, sir?"

"Bring it to me in Thomas City." He cleared his throat. "I'll take care of everything. Her mama has passed, so I'll take care of her."

Without another word, he sat down, took up the reins, and slapped them lightly on the horse's butt. The crowd parted to let him through, and he drove slowly out of town.

The road was muddy, cut badly with the hooves of the posse that rode in that morning, so he drove slowly, carefully, trying not to shake Guinn much at all.

He turned to glance at her over the back of the seat. "Are you all right, sweetheart? I know you need to talk about it, and I want you to, but not till we get home in our own place, so you'll feel comfortable."

"Yes, that would be good. I'm not so sure I can talk about it, even after we get home."

"You can talk about anything under the sun you want to me. Just close your eyes now and relax. We'll be home in no time."

He might let loose and cry yahoo except just because he'd found Guinn didn't mean she was safe from suffering. No telling what she went through while with those awful men, but he would support her, no matter what.

"Is it true?" Her voice failed her with the question.

"Is *what* true?"

"Rosie's gone? Dead?"

"I'm afraid it is. Lost in the storm last night."

"How did it happen?"

"Do you really want to hear this?"

"Yes. Please."

He took a deep breath, wondered how he could phrase it so she wouldn't get more upset.

Gave up on that. There was no way to tell someone a friend they liked had died or been killed. Besides, right now he couldn't talk about it without a catch in his voice, a knot in his throat.

"Well, sweetheart, I see Rose riding that Andalusian horse of hers right up to our door. By the time we get home she'll be there, standing in the yard waving. That's what I see, not a doubt in my mind."

A warm wind dried the tears that rolled down his cheeks, sitting high in the seat, carrying his dear wife home.

Twelve

In her wind-dried clothes, Rose studied the sun's path for a while. Going from east to west, climbing into the center of the sky. With her back to the scorching hot orb, she peered toward the east. Thomas City lay north along a line near the Red River that marked the border between Indian Territory and Texas. Her wild ride had come near dumping her in the river. The other settlements she knew were spread pretty well to her south, all along a railroad line with some to the west a ways.

Turning a circle, she cursed her inability to tell directions as good as she should, but if she went south, or to the right, she should hit the trail that came out of Carlton and headed due south toward Hawkins Post and Cactus Junction. She could hardly miss the towns and would have to swim the river to mistakenly end in the territory.

If he survived the flash flood, Dell

would've gone straight to Cactus Junction to turn back that gang and find Guinn. Loosening the chinstrap of her dried, mud stained Stetson, she crammed it on her head and took off south, the heat beating down on her shoulders. Her boots were still damp through her socks. It didn't take long for her to wish for that big, long-legged Andalusian she'd left in a barn near Carlton. A time or two, she almost turned around and headed the other way to get him. But she needed to go to Cactus Junction first to check on Dell and Guinn.

Amazing how she'd come up out of that turbulent water. Two or three times she'd been sure she would die. Tossed head over heels, water filling her hat, and dragging her this way and that, before going up her nose, all the while nearly choking her. Time after time, she uttered soft words begging for Dell's escape and that he would find Guinn. She supposed they were prayers but didn't know. She wasn't too well-acquainted with talking to God.

Before Cactus Junction came in sight, she'd done her share of talking to whoever might be listening up there. No one had come along to give her a ride like she'd hoped. The reason was evident when she arrived in town. Nearly everyone in the blamed county had gathered here, filling the streets and boardwalk. Something downright important must be going on. Dear Lord, she hoped someone hadn't died. Especially Dell or Guinn.

She made her way through the crowd to see bodies scattered about on the ground, the undertaker and a couple of helpers carrying them away one by one.

"Say, could you tell me what happened here?" She nudged a man standing on the edge of the bystanders. "Who all got killed?"

He turned toward her. "Some rowdies, real tough bunch rode in and tried to shoot up the town, but a couple of sheriffs and their posse put an end to that notion. You should 'a seen it. Gunfire all over the place. It was enough to make a man want to run and hide."

"Who got killed?"

He touched the brim of his hat, looked her up and down. "Say, ain't you that bounty hunter that dresses in britches? That Rose woman?"

She nodded, stretched to see the bodies left on the ground. No way was she going to learn anything from someone who only asked questions.

"I heard someone say you was drowned. Why they've sent some men out to find your body. Sheriff Hoffman was real upset, but he had to take his wife home."

"They found Guinn?"

"Yep, I heard that were her name. You know the lady?"

Well, the conversation might be lopsided, but she was slowly finding out what she needed to know. The rest of the story could wait. Someone had to ride out and bring those men back who were hunting for her body. Maybe she could borrow a horse from the livery and do it herself. Pushing her way out of the crowd, she bumped into a big man wearing a badge. Her gaze crawled up to meet his.

They both reacted at the same time.

"Dutch."

"Miss Rose." He swept his hat off and beat on his thigh. "You're not dead."

Their stares locked.

"Don't think I am."

He finally found his voice. "But we heard you drowned."

"Almost. They tell me someone went out to find my body. I'll go after them if I can borrow a horse. Mine's in a barn up near Carlton. Left him there during the storm."

"Hope you didn't try to hoof it out through that storm, ma'am. It was a doozy."

Before she could reply a young man with

blood on his hands and shirt touched Dutch's arm. "One of them rowdies we put in the jail beat up another of them, and there's blood all over the place. What should we do with them? They're both bleeding like stuck hogs and still trying to go at each other."

"Oh, for heaven's sake." He turned to Rose. " 'Scuse me, ma'am, I have to take care of this. I'll find one of my men to come out and see you get a mount so you can ride after Gil and them. We don't have the men to spare, trying to keep this town settled down and get everything cleaned up and all."

Dutch went after the young man, who had a goodly amount of blood on himself. He must've waded into the fight. She shoved her way down the boardwalk, pushing aside men arguing, others reenacting the battle with words, and clusters of women, some crying, others holding their children close. Older children played about underfoot with no visible discipline, darting between men's legs, running headlong into skirt-clad women, shooting their fingers at each other in battle mode.

Having never been around children, Rose was appalled that little people were turned loose like that. And for them to pretend to shoot at each other, even if only with a finger, disturbed her. In a few years, she'd probably be out running them down, one by one, for shooting up a saloon or robbing a bank. Ah, well, at least she didn't have to deal with them at this age.

She broke loose into the stragglers and made her way to the livery only to find a sign on the door. It read, *Closed.*

Now what? She turned, started for the street again. Coming from the direction of the jail was someone with a familiar face. Drawing closer, she saw it was Lucas, the man who'd been in Dell's posse. Maybe *he* knew someone with a horse she could borrow.

Once more, she had to go through an explanation as to why she wasn't dead, drowned in the flash flood. Then she asked about getting her a horse.

"Boy, that was a doozy, wasn't it?" He stood there, holding his hat by the brim, eyes snapping with excitement. "Sheriff, he took care of business around here, he sure did."

After a moment of silence, she spoke. "A horse. I need a ride."

"Oh, sure. I'm sure we can procure you a mount, ma'am." He grinned great big. "Boy, Sheriff Hoffman's gonna be pleased you ain't drowned. He's been plumb down in the mouth since his wife disappeared, then he thought you'd been carried away by that flash flood."

In about a minute, she was going to run off down the street tearing at her hair. Horses stood everywhere, reins looped over hitching rails. Some appeared to be in better shape than others. Some folks ought to be whipped, the way they took such poor care of their animals. That one over there looked especially good. A long-legged bay, sort of reminded her of Cimarron, except of course it wasn't Andalusian but a nice bay, nevertheless. Looked familiar, but she couldn't quite place from where. She stepped away from Lucas, down off the boardwalk, ducked under the gelding's neck, and ran a hand down his front quarters. He stood, whickered but didn't spook.

Next thing she knew she was on his back and riding through the crowd. What had she done? Stolen a horse. Well, not really. Just borrowed him. It was an emergency, and she'd only need him till she reached the barn near Carlton where she'd pick up Cimarron. She could leave this one there.

Lucas must've gotten tired of talking to himself, for he shouted her name, told her to come back. "I'll find you a good mount, ma'am. I will, just bring that 'un back."

He ran along behind her, waving a hand. "You'll get yourself hung, Miss Rose. Please!"

Someone in the crowd fired a shot. "Oh, shit." She hunkered low. *In for a penny, in for a pound.* She goaded the horse, leaned low, and left town far behind, while several men ran along for a short time before giving up. Slapping the horse with the reins sent him into a long-legged gallop that soon carried her away from those on foot. But it wouldn't be too long before some of them mounted up and came after her. Stealing a horse was right next to cold-blooded murder.

She cut out across the prairie, leaving the well-traveled trail, feeling about as bad as was possible. She'd never done anything so brash, so stupid. If she were lucky, she'd only get hung. But she had to find Gil and then go on and tell Dell and Guinn that she hadn't drowned.

The broiling hot sun that had promised a heat from hell that morning made good on its word. Rose slowed at a spring, got down on her knees beside the pool of cool, clear water and washed her face, neck, hands, and arms. The gelding she'd "taken" wasn't prepared for cross country ride, so the canteen hanging on the saddle horn was almost empty. Thankful she'd noticed, she filled it after drinking her fill at the stream. Tying the wet bandana around her neck, she mounted up and left. Riders would be after her soon.

Though she needed to go to Thomas City and tell Dell and Guinn she was alive, she stayed on the prairie till she reached the barn where Cimarron would still be. Not everyone in Texas stole someone else's horse, and she could count on him being there. No one was home in the house, so she left the gelding in the corral and hurried on out to the barn, swung the door open, and went in to get Cimarron. Surely anyone after her would understand immediately what she'd done and why when they found the gelding there, still saddled, safe and sound and her horse gone. It was plain as the nose on your face.

Only on her way to Thomas City did she remember two things that might mess her up later. She never told anyone she was alive yet, and the stolen horse left at the ranch where they'd originally borrowed fresh horses would sure be confusing for everyone but her. The horse she took in town belonged to a rancher named Daine, who she barely knew from an earlier run in with the man, and she'd left the horse in the barn that belonged to the fellow she and Dell had helped rescue from a fire the year before. Lord, no telling what folks thought other than that she lay drowned in the flood and someone had stolen Daine's horse and left it in that fellow's barn. If she ever got that explained, it'd be a miracle. Well, she'd surely be able to straighten it out when she got to Thomas City.

A horse and rider approached the wagon Dell was taking Guinn home in. He was near where the trail made a Y and the left fork headed for Palo Duro Canyon. He slowed the horse and laid his right palm over the six-shooter on his hip.

Guinn raised her head. "What is it? Are we almost home?"

"No, we're meeting a rider. Lay back down, sweetheart. This will only take a minute."

Getting closer, he recognized the rider. "Hey, Wade. Thought you were in the canyon looking for a clue to the gang. We caught them down in Cactus Junction. The ones we didn't kill are in jail waiting for the judge."

"Who were they?"

"A bunch of wannabe ruffians gathered up by that family whose son I shot a few weeks back. They were convinced they could raid every town along the railroad here in the panhandle and do whatever they pleased. I reckon we taught them different. Only one bad thing, and I hate to tell you this cause I know you and her are, well, were, friends. Rosie Parsons drowned in a flash flood. Just disappeared out from under my sight and was gone, like that." He snapped his finger and thumb.

Wade looked like he'd been shot in the saddle. He jerked up straight then slumped. "My God, when did this happen? Last night in the storms?"

"Yes."

"Have you found the body yet? I can't believe it. Pretty sweet Rosie."

"Not yet. I sent Gil and a couple of the boys out to search for it. Hope it washed up before the floods carried it into the Red. I needed to bring Guinn home after those ruffians mistreated her so."

Wade rode over to the wagon. "Howdy, Missus Hoffman, pleased to hear you're safe. Sorry for your troubles."

A weak thank you came from the form wrapped in blankets.

He backed off. "Well, sorry to hear about Rosie. Damn I'll miss her. Reckon I could go help find her body?"

"Don't see why not. They're searching all along the wash yonder from Carlton. It runs right down to the Red. Thank you for helping. When you find her, would you send one of the men up to the house to let me know?"

"Yes, I'll do that. Rosie's my friend. Of course, I'll help." His voice had a hitch in it when he rode off toward where Dell had indicated.

Dell drove the wagon up into the yard just as the sun set. After carrying his wife inside, he held her hand till she fell asleep. He built a fire in the cook stove and heated water in the reservoir for her a bath. It would make her feel better and sleep easier.

He gazed down at her battered body. In sleep, she appeared so young. He had to awaken her. She would not abide having slept all night in dirty torn clothing without a bath. By the time the water was hot, she was nodding off in her favorite rocking chair. Heaven above. What had she gone through at the hands of those ruffians? They had no mercy.

He poured a bucket of cold water in the tub, then dipped the steaming water from the stove and poured it in till it felt just right. When he touched her arm, she jumped and cried out.

"Bath water's ready. Let's get you undressed."

"I've been undressing myself since I was six years old, Dell Hoffman. I believe I can still do it."

He smiled and helped her torn fingers slide buttons through button-holes, slipped her ripped stockings from her legs after she toed off her shoes, and pulled her underthings over her head.

Holding her hand, he helped her step into the tub. She sighed, closed her eyes, and leaned back. He'd only bathed her a few times in their married life, once after Teddy was born and again after the sweet babe passed. He would do so again. Her soap, which she made herself, smelled like her when he would take her in his arms. Some cactus that grew on the prairie plus a sweet blue flower. When he rubbed it on her wash rag the sweet scent brought tears to his eyes.

He kissed her on the forehead. What had they done to his sweet Guinn? Would he ever dare ask? More-so, would she tell him? His callused hands grew soft in the soapy hot water. He rubbed the cloth gently over her scratched, bruised body, washing every inch as if she were a baby. During the bath, she appeared to be asleep, but when he finished and rinsed her, she opened her eyes and pulled his face down to kiss him. It was the most tender moment he could remember them sharing in all their years of loving each other.

He slid his arms into the water under her knees and arms, lifted her from the tub, and carried her to the bed where he'd earlier spread a towel. By the time he had her dried, she was asleep. He covered her naked body with a light sheet and left her that way, afraid if he tried to put her gown on it would waken her.

Gazing down at her, his pure angel, he wanted, more than anything else in the world to kill the men who'd held her captive and bruised and battered her.

When he was sure she was fast asleep and wouldn't awaken and need him, he lit a lantern and went out to unhitch the horse from the wagon. He spent some time rubbing him down before turning him into the corral. Then he went to the chicken coop and gathered all the eggs that had accumulated while they were gone. That was one of Guinn's projects, the chickens and eggs and the cow too. His neighbor had kept her milked, so he hadn't worried there.

Looking up at the beauty of the stars, he suddenly began to cry, the tears flowing so fast he sobbed like a child.

That night he slept in a chair beside her,

afraid he might have nightmares of killing those bastards and throw himself around.

The sun had lightened the sky when someone rode up, thunked across the porch, and knocked on the door. He came up out of the chair ready to fight, the visions that had attacked during the night fresh in his mind.

"Sheriff Hoffman, hey, Sheriff. You up yet?"

He swung the door open to see Brand. "Reckon if I wasn't, I'd be dead, what with all the noise you made."

"Gil sent me to tell you there ain't no sign of Miss Rose anywhere. If she stayed in the water, she's washed away with the Red River."

Dell rubbed a hand over his face. "A durned pity, that's a durned shame. She was one of the good ones. Reckon we ought to take one of the bad ones to account for her leaving us like that."

"Too bad it don't work that way. Sometimes the good ones are needed elsewhere. To make heaven a better place maybe."

"Well, I thank you for bringing the news. I'll be here for a time with Guinn. You've been a good hand with our posse. I don't suppose you'd consider becoming a deputy for us. We can sure use good men to keep this part of Texas safe for families to live."

Brand smiled broadly. "I do have my little farm, but there are times when there's not much to do. If I could serve just when you need me and not all the time, I might just do that. That is, if it's okay by you."

"We could arrange something, maybe call it part time and pay you for the hours you put in. Fred works that way too. He was town marshal, but it got to be more than he wanted to handle. It gives me extra men only when I need them. Course, we have a town marshal, but his duties are some different from ours."

"Whatever pleases us both, I reckon."

"Well, you been sworn in for the posse, and you have a badge. Come by the office when things are going right again, and we'll get the paperwork done." Dell stuck out his hand and Lucas shook with him.

Dell stood in the door and watched Brand ride away. Dang, he hoped things would settle down for a while. He sighed. He was sure gonna miss Rosie, but he was sure pleased Guinn had been spared.

He was fixing breakfast when some horses rode up, men hollering and laughing, having a blamed good time. His boots thudded when he stalked through the house. "What in tarnation is going on?" Before everyone dismounted, Guinn had joined him, her face a bit flushed. He'd pay for putting her to bed without her gown on. Right now, he didn't care about that.

Gil, Lucas, and four others who had ridden in the posse acted like it was time for a party or something. All talking at once, he could scarcely understand a word that was said.

He held up a hand. "Okay, enough. One at a time. Lucas, you first."

"Miss Rose turned up, Sheriff —"

Gil couldn't hold it any longer. "And she ain't a body she's —"

Another man from the posse added ". . . as alive as you and us."

Dell put an arm around his wife's shoulders. "Ain't that the best news we've heard today? I can't believe it. Where is she? I want to hear her tell what happened and how she escaped those devil waters."

"She's in Carlton, in jail."

"What's she doing in jail?"

"She stole a horse to go back to that barn where we slept and get her own horse. Sheriff, you have to come. She left that horse at the barn in the corral, saddle still on its back. She had no intention of stealing it. She just needed to get to hers. You gotta get her out of jail."

"Well, who put her there? I'm the sheriff of the county. It's my place to jail horse thieves."

"Well, a bunch of those who don't like bounty hunters gathered in the street and demanded she be arrested. I reckon it were Sheriff Runkle who arrested her. Claimed you made him sheriff of Legend county till the next election was called, and he had ever right to do it. We tried to stop him, but he's a tough little bugger."

"Yes, he is that. Look, I'm not leaving Guinn for a while. I left Dutch in charge of Saddler County till she's better. Go see him, explain what's going on down there, and see if he can't straighten it out. I'm sure Sam has a good reason for holding her. But it won't be for stealing a horse. And you can tell Dutch I said so. We ain't hanging no woman in the panhandle. No siree."

At his side, Guinn tugged on his shirt sleeve.

"I'm taking Missus Hoffman back inside where she can rest. Y'all go on now and tell Miss Rosie to come by here soon as she can."

"No, Dell. You go on with these men and take care of business. Whenever would I demand attention from you when you have a county to run?"

He opened the screen door, turned, and waved at the men. "Go and take care of things. I'll be here if you need me."

He ushered her inside. "Nonsense. You come first. There's not a man out there who couldn't do my job just as well as me. Do you want to lie down?"

She sighed, shrugged, and the look she gave him out of the tops of her eyes told him she was exasperated with him. He couldn't help it, though. Dammit, she'd almost been killed, and the thought of living without her was hellish.

"No, sweetheart, I don't want to lie down. Now stop hovering. Shoo, do something." She moved to her favorite rocker, placed so she could see out the window across the vast prairie. "I won't be treated like a piece of fine glass. Only tough women ought to marry lawmen, and I'm tough. You go on and do your job. If I need anything, I'll summon Emma Lou."

Despite the terrible ordeal, her red hair was arranged just so, and she wore a neat blue dress. If it weren't for the bruises on her face and hands, anyone seeing her now would not believe she'd been through something as bad as she had. Yet, she'd break. Sooner or later, she'd hold it all in as long as she could, and it would crack her wide open. Just like fine glass. He had to be with her when it happened.

Though he hated being cooped up in the house all day, he'd stay. "I'll go gather the eggs, and I'd bet old Betsey would be grateful to be milked. I'll fix dinner when I'm done with the chores."

"Whatever you want, dear."

He didn't like that tone one bit, but he'd say nothing. He looked up from the path trodden to the barn for so many years. Off in the distance came a rider, hell bent for leather.

Now what?

THIRTEEN

Last Rose remembered, she stepped off the boardwalk after leaving the rancher's horse at the horse barn and headed up the street toward the sheriff's station. Next, she was waking up behind bars, a lump on her head and not having a clue how she got there. For a while she lay still, waiting for the dizziness to pass. When no one came to explain things to her, she struggled to sit. The cell whirled around her. It must've taken several minutes to settle it down. So, then she waited for a deputy to show up. Explain things to her. No one came, so she waited some more.

What the hell was going on?

Headache gone and done with waiting for someone to come and get her out of this dump of a jail, Rose jumped off the excuse for a bed and strode to the bars. Shook them to no avail, then shouted, "Sam! Hey, Sam. You forget I got you this job. Better come get me out of here before it isn't yours anymore."

She cocked her head, heard only the low rumble of conversation from the other end of the small building. What were those fool men doing? Surely not trying to decide when to hang her for horse thievery? This was ridiculous. She only borrowed the nag, a small replacement for Cimarron. Dang, this was about to be more than she wanted to handle. It'd been one heck of a few days.

"Rose. *Hsst,* Rose."

Who was that? She peered into the darkest corner, saw nothing but a sleeping man in the cell next to her. No windows to let in the light.

"Who is that?" Why was she whispering? "Dang it, show yourself."

"Rose, it's me. Wade. Keep it down, would you?"

"I'll keep it down. I'll cut off someone's ears if this don't stop. Why am I in jail?"

"Didn't no one tell you anything?"

"No, I come back to town from returning that horse and getting Cimarron. I'm looking for you so we can maybe help out catching these owlhoots, and suddenly, bonk, I'm hit from behind and don't know anything till I wake up laying here on this filthy cot. Probably covered in bed bugs or the like.

Get me out of here. Now."

"If you'd hush, girl, I'm working on it. You hollering ain't helping one bit. They're right there in the other room."

"They? *Who* they? The sheriff? You tell him get his butt in here right now. We need to have a little conversation."

"Ssh. You'd best hush up and listen to me for a minute or two. It ain't the sheriff you need to worry about. He's out there trying to settle things down a bit. The town was under attack. Everything's a real big mess. Then this feller comes in complaining you stole his horse. What's that all about?"

She opened her mouth to reply, and the door flew open from the small office next to the cells. In the light stood a huge man nearly filling the opening, a rifle tucked under one arm like he might use it if he had to.

"Deputy James Ellis, ma'am. You need to keep it down so's we can get this taken care of."

"Well, Deputy James Ellis, *you* need to tell me where the sheriff is. He can straighten things out."

"Ma'am?" Ellis slid into the room and pulled the door closed behind him. He unlocked the door to Rose's cell. "I have a complaint from a Mister Daine that you took his horse the other day without permission."

"I did, but it wasn't theft. It was an emergency, and I only borrowed the nag to get on the trail of those ruffians, which I did. Then I took it back the next morning." She looked all around. "Was that this morning? Anyway, I took that blamed nag back. What's the problem?"

"If you'd quiet down, we're trying to get this fixed."

"Fixed? Fixed? How?"

Out of the dark corner, Wade emerged. "Rosie, listen. Right now the onliest thing we can figure to do till this is straightened out so they don't decide to hang you, is help you escape, but you gotta lend a hand so none of these good men are blamed. You and me, we're gonna get out of here. I'm already supposed to be in pursuit of those who escaped from causing all this uproar."

"Pursuit? You can't take them down on your own."

"No, remember, before this attack we was going to sort of join the gang so we could get word back to Dell and his posse as to where the gang would go next?"

Rose listened with disbelief. Obviously, the rap on the head had wiped out some of her memory. If Wade said it was so, then it must be so. "Okay, so just go tell the man I ain't here anymore. I'm already gone."

Wade cleared his throat. "It'd be better if the whole town kind of, well, saw you and me get away. That way it makes it easier for us to get in with them owlhoots we're all hunting. In all the confusion, the horse thievin' charge gets slipped under the rug. 'Sides, he did get his horse back with no damage."

She stared up at the ceiling and grinned. "And this is your big plan? To break me out in front of everyone, then everything will be just fine? We can go on our way. Track those owlhoots, convince them we're being chased by a posse, and —"

"It's a good plan, Rosie, girl."

"Stop calling me *girl,* Wade."

Without pause Wade drew his sidearm. "Back up deputy, right now." He said that like he was play-acting.

Ellis shuffled backward like he believed he was going to get shot. He opened the door and backed into the office, his hands in the air. Wade followed him. Behind Wade, Rose, a bewildered look on her face, went along with it.

Wade made sure he was where he could be seen from outside through the window and shouted, "No one's gonna hang Rose for borrowing a danged horse if I have any say in it."

Rose stifled a laugh as the performance went on. Then she joined in. "Where's my gun?"

Ellis fetched Rose's Winchester from the closet, handed it to her, and looked down at his boot toes.

"Well, it *was* a pretty good plan, throw'd together like it was. You two go on and git after that rowdy bunch, do the job you set out to do."

Wade turned for the door. "Come on, Rosie."

"Wait." Ellis took a step toward Wade. "You gotta hit me first."

Wade stopped dead. "Hit you? I ain't even mad at you."

"It's got to look like I put up a fight so's folks believe it."

Still stifling a laugh, Rose chimed in. "He's right, Wade. If we're going to do this, it's got to look good."

Wade considered for a moment. "Aw, shit." He swung back and threw a left hook that turned Ellis a half circle. "That do it?"

Ellis grabbed his face where it hurt. "Yeah, go on, get out of here."

Wade grabbed Rose's hand, and together they hurried out. Their horses were tied in front of the jail, and without delay they mounted, him leading the way in which the gang had headed earlier. Rose glanced back to see Ellis rush out of the office, making all sorts of gyrations, to get folks' attention.

This better work.

"Are you sure you aren't tired, sweetheart? We've been out here on the porch for hours." Dell kissed the back of his wife's hand.

"If you don't stop babying me, I swear I'll send you to town to shop."

He laughed, and she joined him. Though the bruises on her face and the cuts on her arms and legs were still evident, they were healing. She sat in her favorite rocker which he'd carried outside. She put her favorite pillow in it to make it more comfortable.

"I want to make sure you're all right."

"I am all right. Tell you what. In the morning, go fetch Emma Lou to spend the day with me, and you go in to work."

"Aw, honey, I don't want to leave you yet. What if you fell or something?"

With a huge sigh, she kissed his cheek. "Dear heart, there's no reason for me to fall. I'm not an invalid, but I will be soon if you don't go on back to work and let me start doing mine. I miss my chickens and milking Old Boney and cooking and cleaning. Please."

"Okay, tomorrow first thing, I'll ride over and see if Emma Lou can come stay with you. That's the only way I'd leave you here alone. They've got those evil doers in jail, or I wouldn't go."

The idea terrified him. When he'd seen her beaten and tied, he'd wanted to kill someone. Still did when he thought about it. But she was right. Neither of them could live always anticipating something bad happening. That was no life. So, he would get back to business tomorrow. Dutch was supposed to bring Rosie over here from the jail in Carlton. Idiotic for Sam to arrest her for borrowing that horse. But he trusted Dutch to get it straightened out. When he retired, he hoped Dutch ran for sheriff. That wouldn't be for a while, though.

Guinn rocked, her eyes closed while she hummed a favorite hymn. He'd go to church with her Sunday, her first day back after she'd been stolen. Sundays were for church and fishing.

He leaned back and stared out across the prairie. Something moving off out there. Too far to discern what or who it was. Coming from the direction of Carlton. Dang, he sure hoped it was Dutch bringing that gal back. He worried about her. Soon the riders came in sight, and sure enough it was Dutch, Rosie, and a stranger. Once they got close, he saw the stranger was that outlaw, Wade Guthrie, Rosie was so crazy about. Too bad she couldn't settle on some upstanding young man, but he could hardly criticize her. She ran with the roughest, so it followed she'd be attracted to one.

The wind caught his hat when he went down the steps to greet them. Having dismounted, Dutch chased it down and returned it to him.

"Get down and come on in, all of you. It's cooler in the house. Guinn, look who's here."

He opened the door and invited them in. Draperies covered the windows to keep the sun out, and the dark rooms were indeed cooler than outside. Guinn rose before he could go to her and followed them inside.

"Good to see you feeling better, Guinn." Rose walked along beside her.

"Dell, there's lemonade or coffee in the kitchen. Would you mind?"

He broke off before asking for an update on Rose's arrest and fetched glasses of the tart drink for everyone.

When they were all seated, the subject came up. "I want to know everything about

Rose being arrested for stealing a horse." He eyed Dutch. "I can't believe that happened in Sam's county."

Dutch shook his head. "That James Ellis is the one who done it. Sam was still away from the office handling all those ruffians they arrested tearing up Ned in Carlton. Ellis is an asshole, but he stepped up. I understand he helped get Rose away by taking a sock to the jaw. He's been prone to sit around with his feet up when there are prisoners to tend to and paperwork to do. Reckon he felt bad or something, 'cause when Sam came back to find Rose had been in jail for horse theft and James nursing the lump on his face from Wade breaking her out, no one could've been more surprised."

Guinn interrupted the flow of conversation. "Wait a minute, how could anyone accuse Rose of stealing. I don't believe it for a minute."

That complaint was what was bad. This fellow definitely had an axe to grind. Dell would have to get it quashed somehow to keep her from being arrested or a wanted poster circulated. It'd be best if she went somewhere out of the panhandle, maybe even deeper into Texas, until he could get this nasty situation untangled. But he didn't want to go into it with these fellas or Rose.

The less they knew about what he was going to do, the better it would be.

He leaned forward in his chair. "Tell you boys what's got to happen while I get this handled. Rosie, you have some relatives in Colorado, don't you?"

Rose, who had been silent while the others discussed her experience, nodded, still holding her silence. Probably a bit embarrassed by the entire thing. Wade had squatted on the floor beside the chair she sat in. His expression was one of dismay as Dell went on.

"Don't even go to town where you've been staying. I can get a deputy to go with you if you'd like, but you need to go on up there for a few weeks till I can handle this nonsense."

"I'm not sure about that." Rose finally broke her silence. "The only family are some cousins who I haven't seen since we were young. I wouldn't know them. They wouldn't know me."

Wade rose from the floor. "Sheriff, I can keep her hid away for as long as is necessary. There won't be any problems, I promise, if you let her go with me."

Rose came up out of her chair. "Excuse me, fellas. I know you all mean well, but I haven't had a keeper since I was fourteen.

I'm capable of staying hid on my own. And you can all stop worrying about me. When are those fellas going to be tried?"

"Judge Heller will be through our district in a few weeks. I'll wire him and let him know about the arrests, so he can put us on his schedule. I doubt Sam has done that, since he's not acquainted with all our regulations yet.

"Rosie, just in case they bring that arrest warrant up before him, it'd behoove you to stay away from the panhandle while he's here for sure."

"Okay, Dell, but I don't believe Daine is going to carry through with any plans to get back at me."

He looked her up and down. "Well, girl, if you can make yourself invisible during that time, I'll be one amazed man."

"Sometimes doing that calls for extreme solutions — which aren't always exactly legal."

"As long as you don't get caught." There, he'd said it and surprised himself as well as her. He obeyed the law, often argued with Rosie when she wanted to blast right on into something that was illegal.

But during this long posse hunt, he'd seen what this gang could and would do. He had to reconsider the structure of the law. That they had kidnapped Guinn, then tore up a town in broad daylight with residents looking on and no lawmen able to corral them, he had to reconsider his staunch defense of every law. Too often outlaws got away with whatever they wanted without fear of being arrested.

She gaped at him. "Break the law as long as I don't get caught? I'm amazed, Dell."

He shrugged. "Well, some laws tend to punish the innocent. To say you stole that horse is ridiculous, yet it's the law. And, by God, it's not right. You could have used better judgment, but your intent was perfectly within the law. I'll do my best to get the charges dropped, then you can come back. Where can I locate you to let you know?"

"I'll be across the border in Indian Territory. There's a few faces on wanted posters I figure are hiding out over there. I'm going to do some hunting of my own till this blows over. I'll be in touch." She gave him a hug and kiss on the cheek. "Take good care of yourself and Guinn. I'll be seeing you."

Rose went around telling everyone goodbye.

She left with everyone wishing her good luck. Dell had a bad feeling about her hunting in Indian Territory. He gestured to Wade, guided him out into the kitchen out of Guinn's hearing.

"I don't care what she says, that ole boy whose horse she took evidently has it in for Rose and was just waiting for a reason to get back at her. It'd be quite a coincidence — unless she deliberately took that particular horse, that is."

"I wouldn't put it past Rose if she was pissed at him about something. You know how she can be? But I don't think she expected him to react so harshly."

Dell peered out the window, then turned back to Wade. "Whatever it is, I'd sure like to know, so we have some ammunition. You might nose around and find out what his motives are."

Wade nodded. "I'll do my best, Sheriff. But you know how danged secretive she is."

"Yeah, we're going to have to dig into his past to learn what it is. Keep in touch. And if there's anything I can ever do for you, let me know."

Wade nodded, went to the back door, stepped out, and soon the sound of horse's hoofs pounding the dirt announced his departure.

Strange man, just came and went without even a fair-thee-well. Wonder how him and Rose became friends. Him an outlaw and her a bounty hunter. He'd hinted at being curious about the man to Rose a couple of times, but she didn't give him a reason for the friendship.

But what the hell was going on outside now? Was Rose coming back, or was that someone else riding in hell bent for leather? He rushed through the house and back outside. The rider came right up to the porch where everyone was gathered.

"Sheriff, Sheriff. You gotta come quick. Someone gunned down Gil right in the street in front of the sheriff's office."

Face red with perspiration, Deputy Brand leaped from his horse and stood panting at the bottom of the steps.

"Who was it? Are they dead?" Dell looked all around like he couldn't figure out what to do. In truth, he didn't know what was best to do, at least for an instant. Leave Guinn here? With that wild man and one of his sons still on the loose? No siree.

"We got a wire off to the Rangers before we got sure everyone was safely hid. I have to git on back to help out."

"Hurry on then." Dell turned to his wife.

Guinn rose from the rocking chair. "Stop at Emma's and have her come on over."

But that wouldn't be enough when he had no notion who was involved. What if they took Guinn again?

Brand scuffed boots in the dirt. “Go on, Sheriff. I’ll stay here with the Missus and make sure no harm comes to her.”

Dell spared a quick glance at his wife, she nodded, and he gave her a quick kiss before running around to the barn to saddle Curly. The devil himself was on his trail all the way back to town.

Fourteen

The wind blew so hot the very gates of purgatory must be open straight into hell. If Rose were judge, there were a few people she'd send through. Like those who made it impossible for her to remain here. The last thing she wanted to do was leave the panhandle. At least not under the accusation of horse thievery. She hated to admit it, but she only took that particular horse 'cause she recognized the brand and knew the owner. They had a past she didn't regret. Obviously, *he* did, though, or he wouldn't have taken it upon himself to accuse her of stealing the nag. Perhaps he did so just to get her attention. Well, he'd done that much. So, before she took off like a scared rabbit, she was going to see him. No doubt that was all it would take to get him to withdraw the complaint. And that would be the end of that. Or the beginning of something between them. Who knew?

Matt Daine's Bar 10 Ranch was southwest of Thomas City, right square in the center of the panhandle, about halfway between Amarillo and Lubbock. What he was doing in Carlton the very day she needed a horse, though, was a mystery.

She only met him that once. A few years back, she returned from her first manhunt out in New Mexico. Weary and thirsty, she stopped and spent the night in the bunkhouse on his ranch. It'd still been winter, and the hired hands were all gone till spring. That evening, he joined her on the pretense of building a warm fire for her — which he had done. After spending a fun night together, they parted friendly, or so she believed.

Obviously, something got in his craw to make him swear out a warrant for her arrest when she borrowed his horse. She could only hope it was a ploy to get her attention. She had to find out what it was and get this settled. As good a reason as any to ride over and surprise him. It wouldn't take much to talk him into withdrawing the charges.

After stocking up on trail supplies in Carlton, she packed them carefully in her saddlebags, filled her canteen at the city well, and rode south out of town without even a goodbye. The trail Y'd in about a mile, and she soon faced a stiff west wind. Cimarron continued to snort and blow, and she didn't blame him. The hot air was dry and dusty. They'd stop for the night along the trail and finish the trip tomorrow.

With an uneventful ride behind her, she rode onto the massive Bar 10 Ranch early the next evening. It took till almost dark to make the ride from the gates to the sprawling house. Behind it at angles were two huge red barns, a couple of sheds, a good-sized chicken pen and house, and another building larger than some peoples' kitchen with a small watering tank on the flat roof.

She rode slowly around the yard, then approached the pillared front porch. The house looked like it belonged in Louisiana rather than the panhandle of Texas. My, my, he'd come a long way since she'd stopped for water and remained overnight in his arms. Back then it was a log cabin, with a bunkhouse and the skeleton of a second barn partially completed.

Before she could wahoo the house, the door opened, and several rowdy looking cowboys burst out. They hauled up short when they saw her. One turned and went back inside. Soon Matt came out with him. She got down off Cimarron to talk to him.

"Damn, woman. What're you doing out

here?" He said something to the man next to him who came off the steps and grabbed her.

She couldn't shake loose. What was happening? "Matt, I just stopped by for a drink of water. If it's about the horse, you got him back in good shape."

"Oh, you rode miles off the trail to stop for a drink? Or maybe you want to talk about that horse. I don't think so."

"Of *course,* I want to talk about the horse. What else? What's going on? I don't understand." Surprised, she struggled and kicked to get loose.

"What now, Boss?" The guy holding her tightened his grip on her wrists.

"Take her to the back room and tie her to the bed for now till I decide what to do with her."

"Matt, what the *hell* is going on?"

"You came to the wrong place at the wrong time. Who sent you, bounty hunter? You surely didn't expect to haul us all in, did you?"

Two men dragged her up onto the porch and inside. Her struggles only made them hang on. She obviously had arrived at the wrong time. Whatever was going on, she'd best settle herself down till she could get a chance to get away. Whatever they were up to, it had to be against the law.

She spent the night tied to the bed. Didn't help her sleep one bit, her arms stretched tight above her head and feet wrapped in a rope that held her legs in one spot all night. Nothing comfortable about that. So, as a result, she was awake when a bunch of them rode out, leaving the place pretty quiet.

Wonder what they did with Cimarron. If they made him hang around out front saddled and bridled, she'd see the bastard paid big time. Bad enough tying her this way, but there'd be no forgiveness if he did the same to her horse. Wonder what they were up to going off in the middle of the night like that.

She jerked hard on her arms. One of the rods connecting the top to the bottom of the head of the bed wiggled. After a long struggle and very sore wrists, she managed to get it loose enough to turn. If only the top bar could be shoved upward. One hand cupped under it, she lifted. It moved. Another shove, it moved some more. The ropes cut her wrists till they were bloody, but she ignored that to concentrate on shoving upward. Almost. Her arms ached, so she relaxed a while.

She must've fallen asleep because she awoke to the noise of the men returning. The sun peeked into the windows, and she still wasn't free. They came in whooping and hollering. Drunk, no doubt. Once they quieted down, she went to work on the bed again.

It must've been near noon with the sun high in the sky when the rod came loose just as the bedroom door came open, and in he came. Her heart practically choked her. If she wasn't supposed to still be tied, she'd have hit him with something, but it was prudent to wait for the right moment . . . and maybe see what the hell he was up to.

He carried a steaming cup and wore a wide smile. Heavens, that smile. He was still one good looking man, though the past years had taken a toll on his appearance. Gray hair at the temples, and plenty more wrinkles around his still luscious mouth aged him.

"Look at you, darlin. How long's it been? Five years? Six? I've missed your pretty face."

"Turn me loose and you'll see I'm more than a pretty face. And I don't need that unless you're going to let me go first. I'm liable to soil your bed if you don't."

That laugh she remembered was now tinged with a cruelty she'd never noticed before. "If you hadn't stole that horse of mine, you wouldn't be in this predicament now."

"If you hadn't pressed me about it, had a warrant put out, neither of us would be in this predicament."

He raised an eyebrow. "Oh, what makes you think I'm in trouble?"

"Do you really think I won't be missed? They're looking for me already."

"They? *Who* they? You place a lot of importance on yourself. Just who do you think might be looking for you?"

"I told Sheriff Hoffman where I was going. He let me loose if I'd promise to come back with your release of the warrant on my head."

For just a moment he looked concerned but managed to hide it quickly. "Why would he do that?"

She shrugged. "Maybe he likes me."

"Bullshit, woman. You're trying to get under my skin."

"No matter. He'll be here with a posse to take me back either way. So, whatever it is that you're up to around here, you can kiss it goodbye. And all you had to do was rescind that complaint. Now you're in a heap of trouble."

"Thanks for the warning."

He turned and hurried from the room.

Her and her big mouth. She should've kept it shut till she got free. Untied wasn't exactly free, but, no, she had to show him he was beaten. Well, he really wasn't, not yet. Still, the odds of her getting out of here looked better. She went back to work on the loose rod, slipped one tied arm loose, then the other, then the legs. Noises within the house, the sound of someone coming, and she scrambled off the bed, shoved the window open, then rolled onto the floor and under the bed just as the door was shoved open.

Boots stomped across the floor. "Hellfire. She's gone out the window." Some more stomping. "Anyone see her? Git after her. She'll go for that horse."

She waited till their noisy departure faded, then slid out the window to the ground. She no more than turned to run when a hand cupped over her mouth, another wrapped around her chest.

Dell drew up short of riding through town and stopped at the livery. Joe came running out.

"Sheriff, you going after them?"

"I need a big favor. With Brand at the ranch protecting Guinn and Gil gunned down, the only sworn lawmen I have available are Dutch, Fred, and Guy, plus town marshal Whit Burns. Fred being part-time and Guy the jailer, only Dutch has any real experience as a deputy going face to face with outlaws. Whit could always step in, but he's no gun hand either. Among them I've only got a couple real gun hands. There was a time when you —"

Joe shook his head, hung thumbs in his belt. "Sorry, no sir. I've killed me my last man. You know I give that up when I shot that boy. He hadn't done nothun', but I was so blessed sure. I've not been punished, and I cain't go back on my word. It's mine to keep."

The words tore at Dell. He'd killed a boy, too. That's what had caused all this uproar. He knew exactly how the other man felt.

He tipped his hat. "I understand, I truly do, just be careful to not get yourself killed when this bastard busts into town, 'cause he will cut you down where you stand. You and those you love. I'm sorry this shit-storm has hit, and I feel partly responsible. But when something like this happens, and push comes to shove, it's the man causing it who's responsible. I keep telling myself that. He needn't pick up a gun and come hunting, nor should he have taught his sons to do the same. It'll get them all killed. And by

God and thunder, they'll be responsible, not us who stood up for our own."

Joe nodded, looking miserable. "I hear what you're saying, and I know you're right, but when I pick up a gun and aim it all I see is that boy's face right before my bullet found a way to him. And then, God help me, after. 'Cause of that I got no family for this one to go after. I purely detest anyone like him, but I can't take up a gun again."

Dell frowned and nodded. "I'll talk to some of the other men in town, warn them he and his boys are coming back to finish what was started here. He's vowed to get me, has already hurt my wife. If it comes to it, would you allow the women and children to come here and hide before he gets here with his murderous heart?"

"Of course. They can hide in the hay mow. As long as they're quiet up there, he'll never find them."

Dell nodded. "I'll pass the word. I thank you."

Fleece Jones and the Mercantile owner, Ivan Relenski, agreed to stand with Dell, as did the banker, Dean McIlroy, who, despite his age, patted the barrel of his shotgun and said he welcomed excitement once in a while to start his blood to flowing good again.

Dell sent the available men to hide on rooftops on each end of town and at needed lookout points elsewhere. There hadn't been time to replace the busted windows from the first attack, but for the most part, they were boarded up. His advice — don't hide behind those because bullets would cut right through them. Everyone was advised as to the best place to be to protect their own property, women and children rounded up and taken to the livery. All was ready.

And they waited. The town appeared to be deserted. No one walked the streets or did their shopping. No children played outside the schoolhouse, thus no shouts of joy. Only the wind walked down the streets stirring up dust devils. It was like the place had died.

Along about supper time, a shot cracked open the deathly silence. Just one, and it came from the southern point where Frank and Fleece Jones were stationed. Dell had warned the men not to all run to wherever shots were fired. It could be a trap to get them away from one of the targets. "So, stay put, whatever you do. I'll pick a runner to check out anything suspicious."

In the end, he chose himself for that job, and so he hurried along behind the main street buildings to the corral and back entrance of the livery. Had they known the women and children were hidden there?

He sneaked through the back door, careful to announce his arrival to Joe before the man could turn and shoot him. "Where'd that shot come from?"

Joe shrugged. Pointed. "Somewheres out back, but when I looked, there was no one there."

"They're trying to draw us out, cut us down one by one. That must mean there aren't many of them, or they'd ride in shooting. Stay put for now."

He slipped back outside. The town could sure use some help about now.

Like he'd made a wish, the thunder of hooves approached along the main trail. Hard to tell if it was help for him and the town's defenders or outlaws who could take advantage of a good thing. He hurried up the alleyway under Doc's staircase and hid there waiting till the riders passed by. Sunlight sent slivers flashing off badges hanging on their pockets or at their waist.

The stars of Texas Rangers.

It'd been a long time since he wore one, but he wouldn't ever forget those days.

Shouting, he ran out into the open, rifle held above his head. "Take cover, take cover."

Dust rose in a thick cloud when the horses came to a fast stop. Rangers hit the ground running in all directions, a couple of them joining Dell where they all took cover under the staircase.

"What's going on here? We got a wire calling for help. It took a while to gather enough of us, then here we ride into a dead town."

Dell introduced himself and quickly explained the situation. "We've got all the women and kids and old folk who were in town today hid out in the livery. All others are armed and waiting for these killers to hit."

"I'm Ranger Norton." They didn't bother to shake hands. Norton went on. "He must be something for y'all to prepare like this."

"We expected him to bring along a gang. Word's out he's got a big one that's taking over towns. They tried it in Carlton, broke out window glass, stole merchandise, and emptied a saloon a while back, only to leave a warning they'd be back to collect protection money, so we're not just going by word. We don't understand how something like this can happen, but my deputy is shot and up at Doc's, so we figger they're on their way."

"Heard tell someone stole your wife. These the same ones?"

"It would seem so. But that was a clear case of revenge. His boy drew down on me, and I shot him." He shook his head. "Bad thing to happen, but anyone with a gun pointed at me, and I don't hesitate."

The ranger studied Dell for a long moment. "You got men at both ends of town?"

Dell nodded.

"Okay, let's divide and conquer. Clean this up before the rest of 'em get here."

Dell was happy to let the Rangers take over, and they soon swept from one end of town to the other, going through stores in groups until it was assured whoever had shot Gil was long gone, and no one else was there. All the citizens were sent home and stores shut down.

Later at the sheriff's office, lawmen filled the room, murmuring to each other when Dell returned from checking on Gil's condition. "He'll be okay. Thinks he shot the old boy who called him out. Remembers seeing the second one half-dragging him to his horse before passing out in the street."

"Did he recognize them? Was he able to place them as a part of this gang that hit Carlton?" Norton stared out the window.

"Yep. He said they were the two boys of the three harassing folks along the trail a while back and who came back later with a big gang of ruffians." Dell stared past the gathered Rangers out the window onto the street. "I killed their brother when he drew down on me out there. That's what started all this. I have no notion if it's connected to the gang raping the panhandle."

Or to Rosie's problem. He kept that thought to himself. Why in the hell would Matt Daine, the owner of a huge — and very successfull — ranch, be involved in a gang stealing and destroying towns? That made no sense at all. But it didn't make much sense that the rancher would waste time complaining about such a thing as a borrowed horse that was immediately returned by someone he knew.

He looked around, rubbed his hands together. "Well, we've got a town filled with upstanding lawmen. It's doubtful anyone will try anything tonight."

Norton took Dell aside. "Sir, I'd suggest that first thing tomorrow we hit the trail and try to find this wild bunch."

"I agree."

Fleece Jones stomped up the boardwalk steps with a slip of paper in his hand. "It's a wire, Sheriff. Just come."

Dell grabbed it. "Oh, no. I was afraid of this. They hit Cactus Junction last night. This was all a ruse to keep us looking in the wrong place for them. Ranger, we'd better get over there quick, there's only a town marshal to keep law there."

"Is it a smaller town than here?"

"Yep. I don't know what they'd get there. A mercantile, a smithy, and a livery is about all that's in town."

"Then that could be your ruse, Sheriff. They'd get a lot more here in Thomas City, what with a bank and all these businesses. I'd suggest we send a couple of Rangers and a deputy down there and keep the rest of law enforcement right here guarding this town. And I'd suggest we do it pronto. Send some riders out with them who can circle around and come back. It'll look like we're abandoning the town. Meanwhile, send a wire down to them to Cactus Junction to find out how they fared."

Dell sent a man to the depot to have Fleece send the wire. "And you wait till he hears back, so you can let me know right away."

The man nodded and hurried away.

Two Rangers and Fred Hanks left for Cactus Junction, accompanied by four elderly men who had orders to double back after a few miles. It looked like Thomas City would need all the gun power possible if Ranger Norton was right. If he wasn't, Dell hated to think what would happen down at the junction. At this point, he was glad it wasn't his decision. Worrying about Guinn was about all he could do.

"Where the heck is the man I sent to the depot? He ought to be back by now."

"I'll go and check." Norton trotted off. He returned in a few minutes. "Cain't raise anyone down there."

"Ah, damn." He studied the Ranger, shrugged. "What's done is done, let's get ready for them to hit here. We can't spare any more hands."

The farm they lived on wasn't far from Thomas City.

"I'm going home for the night. Since you're here, I need to see to Guinn. I'll be back in the morning."

Norton nodded. "See to your family, we'll protect your town."

"I thank you." Dell mounted up and headed for home. The old man whose son he'd shot might try once more to grab Guinn. This time Dell feared he'd finish the job and kill her.

It was nearly dark when he rode slowly into the yard. The house was dark. Odd, usually lamps would be lit by now. His heart skittered around as if trying to escape from his chest. Had they already been here?

Perhaps killed Brand and dragged both women off?

Or worse, killed everyone?

He pulled his rifle from the scabbard and dismounted. He should never have left the women here. Leaving Curly to his own devices, he crept around the corner to the back of the house. Guinn's chickens had gone to roost but clucked down in their throats when his boots crunched in the gravel. Keeping his body clear of the door, he went up the steps into the mud room, then opened the door without going in. Just as he slipped inside, someone scratched a match and lit the kitchen lamp. A sulphur odor tickled his nostrils and his eyes, accustomed to the dark, saw nothing for a few seconds but the burning wick. He cocked the rifle. A voice said his name, and breath exploded from his lungs.

"Emma Lou, you scared me to death."

"You did me, too."

"When I saw there was no light. . . ."

"Missus fell asleep on the divan, and I didn't want to awaken her. Then I thought I heard someone and came to look."

"Where's Brand?"

"He's sitting beside her with his gun aimed at the back door. He might have shot you. That is, if you hadn't been you."

He joined her in nervous laughter. "Well, I'm glad I'm me then."

"Me, too, I was afraid whoever it was could hear my heart beating around in my chest like a drum. Let's tell Brand it is you."

"I'm right here." The deputy moved into the glow from the lamp. "Heard you talking."

Emma Lou poured them both coffee, and they relaxed at the table after Dell told them where the gang was. "We still have to watch out. The Rangers think Thomas City is the target because of its size. I came to spend the night, but I'm going back in the morning."

Guinn stood in the doorway. "What about Rosie? Where is she?"

"I'm afraid she's on her way into Indian Territory until the warrant out against her is quashed. The activities of this gang are keeping me from being able to accomplish that."

Red hair tousled, Guinn came to stand by Dell, touched his arm. "I do hope she's okay."

"So do I." He patted her hand. "So do I."

Fifteen

The hand over Rose's mouth, callused and sweaty, tasted bitter but no more than the fear that erupted from her stomach. She almost made it out the window and gone before they caught her. Tingly legs went out from under her, but her captor held her up. Time to kick him now. If only her numb limbs would move.

In her ear, a whisper. "Rose, it's Wade."

She slumped into his arms. "When we get away from here, I'm gonna smack you a good one for scaring me so bad. Then I'll kiss you. How did you find me?"

"Not now. Wait. Take it easy till they all ride off."

She wiggled her toes, moved her arms around. If they were going to run, she had to be able to. Meanwhile, all they did was breathe and wait, her ear pressed against his chest. His heart thrummed.

Finally, the last of the men rode off, hoof

beats fading to nothing.

She couldn't move. "Okay. They're gone. I heard them talking about Thomas City. It's the bank they're after. We'll go back and warn Dell. This is the gang that's raiding the towns. I overheard them bragging this morning about tearing up Carlton and Cactus Junction."

"We have to hurry, beat them there."

"Come on, but be quiet, they might've left a guard here. Cimarron was in the barn, if one of them didn't ride him off." She pushed away. He turned her loose, and she wilted to the ground.

"What's wrong, you shot or something?" He knelt and started patting around on her.

"Stop that. I'm not shot. I've been tied up all night, and my legs and arms are still asleep. Still not sure how you found me here."

"Later." He picked her up and headed for the barn, her hanging on for dear life.

"Don't you dare drop me, Wade Guthrie, or I'll forget how you rescued me. I'd already got myself free and don't you forget it either."

"Course I won't forget it. Why would I?"

" 'Cause you men like to think we women are helpless. And you'd brag about rescuing me."

"Oh, good grief, Rosie, what a thing to think of at this moment. Hush up and let me concentrate on toting you. You're a big girl."

"I believe you could put me down now."

"We're almost in the barn, just hang on and shut up."

She considered walloping him over the head, but he'd probably drop her on purpose then. So, she waited for a later chance.

Inside the barn, it took a minute to adjust her eyes before she found Cimarron in one of the stalls, head hanging over the stanchion, lip curled in a whinny when he saw her.

"You can put me down now."

"Good, I couldn't have lasted much longer."

She ran to let her horse out, found his saddle hanging beside the stall. How thoughtful. By the time she was on his back, Wade rode up to join her.

"Let's go. Hope that nag can keep up with us." She nodded toward his palomino. "I thought only girls in boarding schools rode those golden show-off horses."

"Ha, ha. Don't worry about that." He took off, leaving clods of dirt in his wake.

It was going to be a long ride back to Thomas City, and they'd have to rest their mounts a few times. Long rides across the flat plains of the Texas panhandle on a sunny summer day was what she and Cimarron enjoyed. If only their destination wasn't in such jeopardy, she would like it much more.

Their first stop was at Small Springs. Fresh droppings and muddy water were signs that the gang had stopped there. Not that long ago, either. While the horses drank, Wade filled their canteens from upstream where the spring first flowed from between some boulders. Flowers grew there in abundance, their yellow and blue and red faces forming nature's pure beauty.

Wade plucked a yellow daisy and handed it to her. She tucked it behind one ear under the brim of her Stetson. For an instant, maybe more, the gesture transported her to another life, one she had given up living some time ago. Courting, making love, building a family together. The possibility flitted through her mind with the coming and going of his smile.

Then it was gone, and she was once again the tough, no nonsense bounty hunter in britches with a rifle in her scabbard. And more-so, with a background most men would run from. Why hope for anything more?

Wade touched her shoulder, and she turned to look up at him. He tilted her chin. "Yellow and gold," he murmured, his lips so close she could feel their heat. *Maybe, just maybe.*

With a shake of her head, she asked, "How did you find me back there?"

"Promise me you won't throw something at me?"

"Can't do that, but I'll throw something at you if you don't tell me."

"I followed you when you supposedly took off for Indian Territory." He gave her a look that said, leave it alone now.

She gave him back one much like it and told him it was time to go.

He nodded in agreement, his whisky eyes changing from soft to the sparkle of excitement.

They were alike, the two of them, both living for the ride, the pursuit, one on each side of the law but holding to their own moral beliefs. Best to leave things as they were.

They traveled under a brutal summer sun that climbed to its apex. If you lived in Texas, you learned to handle the heat, the sweat running from around the band of the hat you wore if you didn't want sunstroke, the way your clothes clung wetly to your skin. And you learned that riding created wind that cooled you.

Cimarron easily set a pace he could live with most of the day, but she refused to push him, caring more about his comfort than her own. Wade rode behind her on the well-beaten path that led northeast to Thomas City, his palomino keeping the pace. In a race, the long-legged Andalusian between her legs could outrun anything on the plains, but they had a long way to go, and she held him back.

Why Matthew Daine, owner of the Bar 10, was involved in something as lowly as a bank robbery, she had no idea. More than that, he had ransacked two other towns for little gain. Something else must be behind these raids. Thomas City was the largest and most successful of the three, but none of them, other than being located on a spur with very little train traffic, had much to offer money wise. Even the bank held meager funds compared to cities such as Lubbock or Amarillo.

If Daine expected any gain at all, it was power. Power to control the economy of the area, or something like that. Not a desire to own three little towns in nowhere land. What was really going on here?

Wade rode up beside her. "Shade ahead.

We need to rest them a while."

She came out of her reverie to see the cluster of trees off to the left. Movement on the other side. "Wait, I think we've caught them. We'd best hold up. Maybe they haven't seen us. We don't stand much of a chance against that bunch."

"Whoa. I think they're moving out. They haven't seen us. If we cut east here, we can hit a northern trail yonder and get ahead of them without them ever knowing it."

She lay her hand on Cimarron's shoulder, foaming with sweat. "I'd rather rest our horses in the shade first, then finish the last jaunt that way. We could still get there ahead of them in time to warn Dell and his deputies. I sure hope he has some extra fire power to go against that bunch."

"Me, too, let's go. Our mounts are up for it. We can catch the next shady spot."

She glanced at the trees, saw more movement, like they were settling down for a while. "You're right. They hit the other towns late in the day and spent the night tearing them up. Looks like they're gonna rest a while. We can take this shortcut and be there before them without running out our horses. Let's just walk away and hope they don't see us. Otherwise, we're in for a gun battle we can't win."

She reined the bay off to the right, and Wade followed, both horses seeming to tiptoe as if they got the message to be quiet. Soon they were behind a rise and in the distance a thick copse and the glimmer of water which surely meant shade. It offered both plus a breeze ruffling the small creek formed by a spring. They settled down, leaving the horses to drink and graze while they splashed their faces and wet bandanas to wrap around their necks before stretching out side by side.

Rose fought sleep by talking to Wade. "Can you imagine Daine's surprise when he finds the small, town bank well protected? Hope that ruins whatever he has up his sleeve. He has to be well-off with that huge spread. What could be worth more to him?"

Wade was silent for a few moments, and when she didn't go on, he did. "Railroads." Not a man of many words, he let her mull that over.

"It's just a little thing, runs over into the San Juan Valley in Colorado, then sort of peters out."

"Yeah, but what if it didn't? What if it ran on to Denver or someplace? What would the land around Thomas City and those other little settlements be worth?"

"You mean, if he grew strong enough to drive folks off their land . . . ?"

"No, think bigger. What if he owned the *towns*? He could build hotels, eating establishments, all kinds of businesses that would ship their products by rail. The west has exploded with railroads since the end of the war, and more and more are coming. Just think."

"And why is he robbing the bank? I doubt there's more than a few thousand there."

Wade went silent again. "Not sure yet, but I'll figure something out. It's all just supposing, anyway. What I might do if I were so inclined."

"And here I thought you'd heard rumors or something."

He laughed. "Time we were on our way if we're gonna get there by dark, before those other yahoos do."

He had some imagination. What she wanted was to riffle through Daine's bunch for wanted men she could turn in for a bounty. It was bound to be a good night all around.

That is, till she and Wade rode out, rounded a mound, and found the way blocked by four mounted men, rifles out of their scabbards. Looking mean as if they rode straight out of hell.

■ ■ ■ ■

The next morning, Dell solved the problem of leaving Guinn by taking her to Emma Lou's. He gave both women the order to shoot at anyone who threatened them. If anyone came to harm her, they'd find the farm deserted and her gone. He needed all of his deputies for the fight that was coming. He would protect his town, wished he could've done the same for Carlton and now Cactus Junction. First thing when he rode into town at the very crack of dawn, he went to the depot. Fleece was already there.

Drawing a grateful breath, he went inside. "Good to see you, didn't know if you'd be up this early."

"Yes sir, and I come prepared." He lifted a big Henry rifle from under the counter.

Dell grinned. "Well, that 'un will do 'er. Have we been able to contact the junction yet?"

"No, but one of the Rangers what went down yesterday came back in during the black of night. He was plumb tuckered out and is asleep over at the livery now."

"Well, what news did he bring?" Getting information out of Fleece was like pulling a hook out of a gut-caught catfish.

"Not good. Most everyone hid out and let 'em have at it. Halfway through the night, the ruffians took out, leaving the place in a shambles. Left a note tacked on the board at the depot. Ever one who owns a business are to leave twenty dollars in a envelope ever month, and they'll be bothered no more. Added, those who don't like the deal, they'll drive them out. Said they'd be back for answers in a few days."

Dell sucked at his teeth. "So that's the deal, huh? Wonder if they left the same in Carlton and it got overlooked? Cain't see them not doing so. Or maybe they just thought of it."

Fleece chuckled bitterly. "Reckon they could've just thought of it. What started as a gang raid could make 'em more money than robbing some storekeepers. I could try again to wire the junction."

"Would you do that, Fleece? I'd appreciate it if you could send someone up to the jail house to let me know when you get an answer. I need to get things prepared. Since they rode in toward night at the other places, it might be their plan here. But I'd rather be prepared today just in case."

So as to keep Curly close Dell dismounted out back of the jailhouse. Before he could go inside, a youngster came running fast up the street, bare feet stirring up puffs of dust.

"Sheriff, Sheriff."

Dell shrugged. Wondered if he could take one more piece of bad news. "What is it, boy? What's happened?"

"Mister Fleece. He said tell you all the wires is down. No one is answering up and down the line. We're plumb left in the dark, he says." The boy bent forward, hands on his knees while he panted out more words. "Can't reach Amarillo or no place."

"Good God Almighty. I've taken about all I'll take from these bastards." He touched the boy's heaving, sweaty shoulder. "I apologize for the language, son. You did fine." He dug in his pocket and came out with a four-bit piece. "Here, take this for your good work."

The boy's eyes popped. "Thank you, Sheriff. Uh, what's gonna happen? Are we all gonna get killed in our sleep tonight? That's what some are saying. If that's true, I'd better get this spent down at the mercantile while I'm still alive."

If it hadn't been so close to the truth, Dell would've laughed. "No one's going to die as long as I can help it. But you go ahead and enjoy you some sarsaparilla and horehound candy. You earned it. Then put the rest away for another day."

Behind his desk, Dell shuffled through the latest hand bills and wanted posters to come through the mail drop. This week. It sure was handy to hook that mailbag off the passing train once a week. It beat waiting for a stage to carry it down from Denver sporadically.

He studied the crudely drawn faces on three new wanted posters, trying to decide if he'd seen them passing through. Not that it would matter much. If he had, they'd already be long gone. Rosie was more apt to be able to run them down, seeing as how she didn't have a county to protect.

Dang, he hoped she was doing all right over there in Indian Territory. It wasn't the Indians he worried about so much as the blood thirsty outlaws who took refuge there. The Apache, with the exception of Cochise's small band, were contained down in Florida, and he doubted they would ever be turned loose. Comanche, now there was a dangerous breed, but she knew to steer clear of them. Those innocent looking white men, they'd knife or shoot anyone they took a dislike to, just for the fun of it.

He rose and tacked the new posters on the wanted wall. No use worrying about her. She'd been at bountyin' over five years now and had carried in many a bad man draped over the saddle of his poor horse. He stopped to look out the window down the dusty street. Not many out and about. Scared. He hated that.

Wonder where the Rangers were. He needed to get them organized and ready for the expected raid. Though they were prone to doing their own organizing, he was the sheriff of Saddler County. But those Texas Rangers, now. They beat all. They were technically in charge of the law in the whole gol-darned state, though it hurt to admit it. Sure, no sense in butting heads with them. He'd heard somewhere that they could ride like a Mexican, trail like an Indian, shoot like a Tennessean, and fight like the devil. He'd never thought about them that way when he was a Ranger himself, but now he believed every word of it.

He'd sure need one and all of them to win this battle. They were free to carry out any fight they deemed fit without going to a higher up for permission. That alone made them valuable to him. They'd come to help.

And here they were.

Eight of them striding side by side up the street. Some of them carried Peacemakers, others Henry Rifles or Winchesters. Well-armed, each and every one.

He took his Stetson off the rack, placed it just so on his head, and went out to meet the most famous lawmen in the world. They were an impressive bunch. No uniforms, yet the way they approached in step, they appeared to be a military patrol. Odd, he'd never been so impressed when he rode with them, but he had other things on his mind then.

He greeted Ranger Norton with a handshake and was introduced to the rest. "If we're going to fight together, we should know the names of our comrades in arms," Norton said, going down the line with last names.

Ranger Castillo, Ranger Smith, Ranger Snake Finger, Ranger Richards, Ranger Jackson, Ranger Hertz, and Ranger Hodges.

Each touched the brim of his well-worn Plainsman in a sort of salute. Norton then turned to Dell. "At your service, Sheriff."

He almost saluted but decided not to. "Glad to have you all here. What I need from you is protection from these cutthroat renegade sons 'a bitches, any way you see fit. I'll see my deputies will follow your lead, since you're all more accustomed to battle than they are.

"This bunch've been riding into a town along about dusk, shooting out windows, riding horses inside buildings, destroying goods. Thomas City has a bank, and we expect it to be hit. I've already had the citizenship warned to go home and stay there till this is over. Most of our businessmen and women have chosen to protect their property."

The Rangers had a confab and were soon spreading around town. He made note of where each one stationed himself, so he could best use his deputies, so no one was caught in the crossfire.

Along about suppertime, Mrs. Martinez, who ran one of two eating establishments, drove a wagon down the center of the street. "I have beans and tortillas for everyone who wants them. No charge." The Mexican woman repeated her offer all the way up the street, and men ran out to gather enough for everyone.

The owner of the saloon, not to be outdone, soon came along offering beer to one and all.

"Dear God, it's a street party." Dell ran out to get food for him and the two stationed near him, then told both vendors to get in off the street and take shelter from the battle soon to come.

People never ceased to amaze him. Their resilience and bravery was beyond belief.

And they would sure as the devil need every ounce of everything they possessed to survive against those of a far different breed on their way.

There was apt to be some dying this night, and he hated the thought. But there was nothing for it but to get to it.

Horses approached, running full out.

"Everyone on alert. Make ever shot count."

Positioned on the roof of the jail house, Dell squinted into the street. Six riders approached at full tilt, led by a big Andalusian bay.

He rose, waved his hat. "Hold your fire. Hold your fire." His order went down the line from one station of shooters to the next.

Rosie, Wade, and four strangers reined in at the livery, dismounted, and marched up the middle of the street to the jailhouse. Rose hollered up at Dell.

"They're right behind us, maybe thirty minutes. These here are U.S. Marshals, come to put a stop to town raiding, they said. Where do you want us?"

"Lord, this is gonna be some battle. We got all the lawmen in the country. Roof tops will stop these old boys we figure. We got eight Rangers, you need to go along and fill in the gaps clear down the street."

One of the marshals stepped up. "We hear they're after the bank. Two of us will double coverage there."

He wasn't asking, but, at this point, Dell didn't mind. "Fine with me, sir. Yonder corner." He gestured, and they trotted over.

The rest of them followed Wade and Rose down the street filling in gaps as they went. Dell settled back down.

Those owl-hoots were in for a big surprise. This was going to be one hell of a battle.

SIXTEEN

Rose headed for the millinery where she planned on taking up a post on the roof. The owner was Missus Lillian Cooper, who at age sixty was full of vim and vigor but only knew which end of a gun the bullet came out of. And there she was, officially at her post, as Rose knew she would be, behind the counter of her store with a heavy bolt of lace in her lap.

The frail woman lifted the bolt and swung it. "Just like that, I'll wop anyone who comes in here to take my store."

Even under the dire circumstances, Rose had to smile. "Missus Cooper, you come with me. You and me together, we'll make sure these men don't get into your store."

"Don't you try to trick me into leaving. I'm perfectly able to defend what's mine. I can't afford to lose this place."

"I'm not trying to trick you, Missus Cooper. We'll defend your store together."

She took her arm and helped her stand. "Let's go in the back room where you can keep guard, and I'll go up on the roof. No one can get past the two of us."

Though she didn't release her weapon, the store owner gave in to Rose's coaxing, and she seated her in the work room behind a table where she created bonnets and church hats. She ought to be safe there with Rose crouched behind the false front of the store roof.

With one last glance into the empty street, she climbed to the roof and settled in armed with her Colt Single Action Army .44, the Winchester rifle, and a belt of ammunition. Ready for just about anything.

Anticipating the battle, her heart thudded with excitement. Placing the fully loaded Colt near her hand, she took up the rifle. That meant she only had to carry one caliber of ammunition. A cartridge belt lay beside her. She was loaded for bear. The two-legged kind.

Riding up on those four U.S. Marshals earlier had her heart kicking her chest like a mule, until they identified themselves. Turned out, they came over from Judge Parker's court to arrest several fugitives riding in the gang raiding the small towns along the border of Indian Territory. Most important was the warrant for Matt Daine, who had made himself quite a reputation, forcing landowners to sell out along proposed routes of new railroads. He was now attacking the small towns along those routes to force business owners to sell out to him. That put him at the top of the wanted list. A huge target for the marshals. Daine's bunch had also killed on several occasions, so Judge Parker would be glad to arrange a necktie party for them. A legal one. The marshals were more than happy to lend a hand at Thomas City.

So here they were, participating in the biggest shootout she'd ever been involved in. She'd sure like to collar one of the lesser wanted fugitives for the bounty, but with marshals on the spot, that was doubtful. Still, she was more than pleased to help put a stop to the routing of these outlaws. The irony was the participation of outlaw Wade Guthrie in rounding up this gang. He did, after all, have his moral standards. If there was a recent poster out on him, the marshals might well include him in the roundup.

She hoped not.

Rifle at his side, Dell took a walk up and down Main Street to make one final check of the positioning of every man jack, be they rangers, marshals, or deputies. Despite his low rank in the lawmen present, he felt responsible since it was his county and his hometown they defended. Whoever died this day would be his to bury, so to speak. As he headed back to the jail house, the pounding of hooves shook the ground beneath his boots.

To the Southwest, a bank of clouds, lit by lightning, boiled into the sky as if to witness whatever went down this night. No lamps burned in windows. It was as if the entire town had died. Thin drops of rain spattered his face when he climbed to the roof. Why did it always rain at funerals? Looked like it was going to be a hell of a night with more than one funeral as a result. Be nice if they could call this off for better weather, but that wasn't about to happen.

Wishing he'd fetched his rain gear from his saddlebag, he found himself an ideal spot, lay on his stomach, and propped the Winchester on the framing boards of the false front. Maybe he could make a small enough target to survive this and get back home to Guinn. Still, the important point of this battle was to stop the evil that threatened good people. Some would die in that effort. It couldn't be helped.

The rain slashed sideways with a sudden

wind, and the pounding of the approaching horses grew louder. It was as if they were being overrun by the hounds of hell. Were these men crazy? Even Indians didn't attack at night. It made no sense. Still here they came, and gunfire broke out on the other end of town. At first sporadic, then blasts so continuous as to threaten the thunder. Men yelled, horses screamed, lightning streaked in jagged fingers that lit up the chaotic frenzy.

The only thing townspeople had in their favor was the enemy was all in the street They were all on rooftops, in much less danger of being hit by a stray bullet. The battle slowly worked its way through town until bullets cut at the storefronts only yards away from the jail and bank. Across the street, the marshals and two deputies held fast, but darkness hid its secrets, so it was hard to tell if any of the gunmen had broken through.

It got to where Dell wished for another flash of lightning so he could make out the familiar front of the McIlroy bank. Rain washed at his face till all he could do was aim into the street and keep firing as fast as the rifle would fire. God help him if one of his men took to the street. He wanted to leap to his feet, wave a white flag, and delay the battle till the weather cleared. Instead, he watched for the flash of gunfire below then aimed there and fired back. Men continued to holler, some screamed in agony, horses squealed. A few of those screams came from roof tops where his men held fast. Bullets zinged past his ear, thunked into the boards. The rain settled into a steady pour till he was soaked to the skin.

Behind him echoed the thudding of footsteps. He rolled around just as bullets cut into the roof all around him. Lying on one side, he pulled his handgun from the other and got off a couple of shots before a bullet caught him in the flesh of one arm. For a few seconds, he felt nothing, then the world tilted, and he was staring up into the rain-washed sky, his arm hammered by pain.

Whoever had shot him must've been hit, too, for his groans matched Dell's. They went on and on, growing weaker until a huge gasp cut them off. Dell lay there listening to make sure his quarry was dead or unconscious before he struggled to his hands and knees, recovered his dropped rifle and six-shooter, and managed to prop himself up against the storefront.

Everyone continued to shoot at God knew what. The only targets were revealed by near constant lightning or gunfire from rifle barrels. It seemed forever before shots grew sparse, then someone shouted.

"Hold your fire."

A rolling lightning flash revealed one of the marshals exiting the bank, rifle above his head. "Hold your fire." His voice boomed into the darkness.

Slowly, all the way down the line grew quiet. One or two lonely blasts, and it was over. Hard to tell how many of the gang must've ridden off when they saw they were defeated, but lying there breathing into the pain of his wound, he listened to the harsh voices of lawmen rounding up survivors. Demanding a show of badges as men crawled down from their perches along the street.

Before long, they herded prisoners to the jailhouse. When it quieted below, Dell called out. One of his deputies came up and helped him down and inside where lamps glowed. Doc Kelton was already there at work on the wounded lying on cots in the cells. Brand helped Dell into his chair when he announced his was only a flesh wound, that Doc should see to the others.

Ranger Norton came in, looking like a drowned rat, his Stetson dark with rainwater. "Been trying to check on everyone.

We've got about twelve down in the street. All dead. Once this weather clears, we can sort things out, but I ordered them carried to the livery where I figured there'd be room to store them till morning."

Dell cleared his throat. "Find Daine in the bunch?"

"Haven't found him yet. Maybe the coward rode off right at the beginning when he saw they were beat. But we know who he is and where he'll run to. Your friend, Rose Parsons, clued us in on that. She's down at the millinery calming some of the shop owners, mostly women." He chuckled. "They sure are a chatty bunch. Like a nest of hens clucking around. Say, that Rose is quite the deal, isn't she? I've heard some about her, but we never met till today."

Doc came in, sleeves rolled to his elbows. "I'm seeing to our men first, but there's a couple of them owl hoots whimpering and crying for help. You want me to patch them up?"

A marshal rose from his seat on the floor. "I want to talk to them first. I haven't found Daine in the dead, nor in those we herded in earlier. If that SOB got away, I want to know where he might go. I'll get it out of one of them, sooner or later."

Norton, tired and reluctant to share the

information he'd gotten from Rose, lowered himself into an empty chair and wiped the rain off his hair and face. "Far as I'm concerned, you can have at it. You'd think when we plan a shootout, the weather could cooperate, wouldn't you?"

Nervous laughter went around the room.

One of the marshals joined Dell and Norton and stuck out his hand. "Deputy Marshal Carrington."

They shook all around and exchanged names. "Sheriff, your deputies done real fine. Sorry about that one young man. Didn't get his name, but they moved his body off the street a while ago."

Dell sat up straight. "Anyone know who of our men was killed?"

The few sitting around were all rangers and marshals. The deputies were down in the street cleaning up the town. Dell resented that for an instant, then decided to let it go. These lawmen had come to the town's aid and helped stop a ravaging. They didn't know anyone or feel a desire to carry off dead bodies.

Before he could say anything, though, Norton tried to smooth the waters. "Once the bodies are all laid out, we'll go in and help the marshals identify their wanted."

Dell struggled to his feet, supporting his

injured arm. "I have to go find out who of my men got cut down."

Carrington rose, slapped his Stetson on his thigh, and put it on his head. "I'll go with you, Sheriff. Know how you feel about your fallen deputy."

The tall, sturdy marshal walked beside Dell out into the warm night. The rain had stopped, and clouds parted to reveal an egg-shaped moon. Off to the north, the retreating storm echoed thunder and distant lightning, then moved on its way. The breeze did its part to rid the air of the odor of gun smoke. Dell staggered a bit, and Carrington supported him till he pushed away.

"I'm fine. You know, I've never been shot in all my years serving the law. Had some close calls, but nary a bullet has found my ornery hide till this night. Maybe that'll help me to always remember this experience. Hate that about my deputy. They could all say the same till this night. Whichever one it was, I'll mourn him. I'm just glad we didn't lose any more than we did. I sure worried about Rose."

"Rose? Is that the bounty hunter?"

"Yeah, and I don't know why I worry about her except us men are wired to worry about our women folk, and she's a good friend."

"I've heard of her, never met her till tonight though. She's brought in some tough characters. The judge says he likes the cut of her britches. You know she asked me if there might be someone in that bunch she could collect bounty on, since she did her share of shooting and knew she'd put some down. Women in britches. What's the world coming to?"

Dell stopped to roll a body over with the toe of his boot and stared into the dead face of the father of the boy he'd killed earlier. "I'll never understand what makes some folks turn to evil like these." He shook his head. "That boy I shot — this is his daddy. He egged the boy on, and after he drew down on me, and I had to defend myself, he tried to blame me and get his other three boys to step in." He moved around the body and headed toward the livery. No sense in telling the marshal all they'd done to his Guinn. The man had paid and now laid there dead and probably did his boys too.

Brand and Fred carried a body past them before they got there.

Dell hurried to catch up. "Say, Brand. Did you find one of our deputies shot dead?"

"I sure did. Awful sorry, Dell, but it was Dutch. He took a bullet to the throat and bled to death. Nothing anyone could do about it."

Dell sure hated that. "He was a good man. Do you know, are the rest of them okay?"

Brand and Fred lay the body down alongside the others lined up on the hay-strewn floor of the livery. "Far as I know. We haven't come across any of the others so far."

"Well, check the roofs, that might be where they are." Dell stared down the street where several bodies still sprawled in their death throes. "These can lay till all the men holding the town from the rooftops are accounted for. God damned shame." He shook his head. "Dutch. A nice, capable man, a deputy who never hurt anyone, even carried out his sworn duty with respect."

Brand and Fred nodded. "We been checking there as we go. We'll do like you say, Sheriff."

The two hurried to the roof, and Dell nodded. He sure hated to hear the final count on the men shot this night to protect the town.

"Since we're here, let's check the bodies. Someone needs to keep track of the dead. Reckon Doc will do that for the dying." Dell shoved open the livery doors, stepped back, and let Marshal Carrington through first, then he followed him into the darkness.

■ ■ ■ ■

Three weeks later, Rose returned from a visit to Judge Isaac Parker in Ft. Smith, Arkansas. She rode up to the front porch of Dell and Guinn's farm outside Thomas City.

The couple greeted her warmly and invited her inside where Guinn had prepared supper. At the table, surrounded by the delicious fragrance of fried chicken and all that went with it, Dell could not hold back his questions any longer.

"Tell us what it was like, visiting with The Hanging Judge."

Rose grinned great big. "He told me he liked my britches and hoped, in the future, women would see their way clear to kick away the traces that bind them, just as I have."

Guinn laughed. "He didn't."

"Oh, yes, and he awarded me with bounty for five of the thirteen men and the marshals hauled over to him. Said if he had his way, U.S. Marshals would be awarded the same bounty money that I was paid, rather than their paltry dollars per trip paid for their work."

"What did you tell him?"

"Oh, I whole-heartedly agreed with him, but I told him it would be a long, long time before all women wore britches."

"You know what, Rose?" Guinn rose and took more biscuits from the warming oven.

"What?"

"I think I'd like me a pair of those. I can see they'd come in handy for gardening and squatting down to milk Old Boney."

Rose regarded the beautiful red-haired wife of her friend, Dell. "Let's go shopping this week. I'll help you find a pair."

Dell smiled at his wife, then glanced toward Rose. "Is the judge going to hang Matt Daine and his crew?"

"It looks like he may. The trial for him and the four surviving members is scheduled for next week. What with the killings they're responsible for, I can't see he'll do any less."

"I heard the marshals caught up with him hiding out in Indian Territory, and he'd already started to organize another gang." Dell buttered another biscuit.

"Oh, yes. That man is incorrigible. Judge Parker will surely do no less than hang him, at least. He may put the others away for a good long while."

"I wonder, Rose. Do you know what happened to the youngest boy who survived the shootout? You know, the brother of the boy I shot."

Guinn's eyes teared up, and Dell took her hand and kissed it before lifting his glass of iced tea. She was no doubt thinking of her sweet Teddy, cut down by the cholera before he could grow up.

Rose licked her lips and looked down, unable to meet the sad eyes of her friend. After losing their only son, the couple had not been able to have any more children. Shooting the young man had weighed heavily on Dell's mind, but surely they weren't considering taking in the younger son. After the way he'd been brought up so far, he would be a handful. It was none of her business though.

"He was the only survivor of his family. The mother died several years ago. I think he went to a boy's home around Fort Smith somewhere. He was only ten and already quite a tough boy."

"Do you happen to know the name of that home?"

"No, but I'm sure it wouldn't be hard to find out. Are you two considering . . . I mean, do you realize he could already be bad?"

Guinn patted her lips with a napkin and rose. "I have a blackberry cobbler. Who wants some?"

After passing around bowls of cobbler and a pitcher of thick cream from Old Boney, talk turned to other subjects. Namely the repairing of the towns along the small railroad that would soon be lengthened to Amarillo on one end and Denver on the other. Everyone could soon look forward to a more prosperous future.

"You'll be needing some more deputies for the growing county," Rose told Dell between bites of the delicious cobbler. "You ought to hire Wade. Ever since fighting on the proper side during the recent battle, he's reconsidered remaining an outlaw. Since he's never killed anyone, and hardly ever kept more than a few dollars of everything he stole from carpetbaggers, who everyone knows are thieves in their own right, he'd make a good one. He's a fine gun hand."

"Have him come around. I'm thinking the town can afford two or three more. Of course, we need to replace Dutch. I had hired Gil after he rode in the posse and did such a heck of a job, and he's agreed to stay on and Lucas as well. I look for this town to grow by leaps and bounds with the increase of the railroad, and with progress comes more lawbreakers to deal with."

Boy howdy, the West was growing by leaps

and bounds. Even the panhandle with its wide, open spaces and dry hot climate attracted both farmers and ranchers. The two seldom got along, considering barbed wire versus free range and cattle stomping crops. That would be one of the problems his department would have to handle in the future.

Though he never thought her the type to settle down to one man, Dell couldn't help but see the way she acted around the young outlaw. He'd need to stop thinking of him as an outlaw if he hired him as a deputy.

Rose left soon after supper to meet Wade at the Golden Triangle, a fancy new saloon in town. He heard it was attracting a lot of attention from those not known to frequent the wilder establishments. Something about a stage and high-class dancing girls.

He sat on the front porch, staring out across the wide prairie. The tall grasses blowing in the wind appeared to be doing a dance of their own. To the west, the sky flared with reds and golds while the sun slipped beyond the horizon and to the east a few stars twinkled. That boy, the one left without any family at all, now he couldn't help but worry about what would become of him without any guidance.

Behind him the screen door slammed, and

Guinn stood at his back for a moment, one hand on his shoulder.

"He would be five this year, our Teddy." Her low voice held a sob.

"Yes." He paused, pulled her hand forward to kiss the palm. "You thinking of that other boy? The one I orphaned."

"That wasn't your responsibility, but I was thinking of him."

"He's had a rough life. He'd be a hard one to handle."

He could hardly try to dissuade her. Doing something to make up to that boy what he'd caused to happen to him ate at him like a dog chewing at a bone, yet he didn't want to talk her into anything she didn't want to do. It was a terribly hard decision to make without asking her to make it too.

She moved around and sat in her rocking chair next to him. For a long while, she held his hand, stared across the prairie, and rocked. Then she turned to him, strands of red hair blowing across her face. Tears stood in her eyes, but a smile played at her lips. She brushed the stray locks back.

"I think we should do it."

He smiled. "So do I, sweetheart. So do I."

ABOUT THE AUTHORS

Dusty Richards grew up riding horses and watching his western heroes on the big screen. He even wrote book reports for his classmates, making up westerns since English teachers didn't read that kind of book. His mother, though, didn't want him to be a cowboy, so he went to college, then worked for Tyson Foods and auctioned cattle when he wasn't an anchor on television. His lifelong dream, though, was to write the novels he loved. He sat on the stoop of Zane Grey's cabin and promised he'd one day get published, as well. In 1992, that promise became a reality when his first book, *Noble's Way,* hit the shelves. In the years since, he's published over 160 more, winning nearly every major award for western literature along the way. His 150th novel, *The Mustanger and the Lady,* was adapted for the silver screen and released as the motion picture *Painted Woman* in 2017.

In a review for the movie, *True West* magazine proclaimed Dusty "the greatest living western fiction writer alive." Sadly, Dusty passed away in early 2018, leaving behind a legion of fans and a legacy of western writing that will live on for generations.

Velda Brotherton wrote from her home perched on the side of a mountain against the Ozark National Forest. Branded as Sexy, Dark and Gritty, her work embraces the lives of gutsy women and heroes who are strong enough to deserve them. After a stint writing for a New York publisher, she settled comfortably in with small publishers to produce novels in several genres and mentor scores of up-and-coming writers before passing away in March, 2023.

The employees of Thorndike Press hope you have enjoyed this Large Print book. All our Thorndike Large Print titles are designed for easy reading, and all our books are made to last. Other Thorndike Press Large Print books are available at your library, through selected bookstores, or directly from us.

For information about titles, please call:
(800) 223-1244

or visit our website at:
gale.com/thorndike

www.ingramcontent.com/pod-product-compliance
Lightning Source LLC
Jackson TN
JSHW020810250725
88263JS00006B/42
* 9 7 8 1 4 2 0 5 2 7 0 6 3 *